'I adore hunting through the French brocante markets and this book will certainly add a whole new dimension to the experience. An entertaining read for anyone interested in antiques or France.'

Judith Miller, founder of *Miller's Antiques Guides* and antiques specialist on the *Antiques Roadshow*

'What a delight it is to be invited back into the world of Serge Bastarde – now with an equally roguish son in tow. From cupboards that crunch in the night, to the reasons why French people love floral china, this book is full of warmth, humour and colourful characters. John Dummer gives us a real insider glimpse into the world of the French antique markets. Don't go near one until you've read this book!'

Karen Wheeler, best-selling author of *Tout Sweet*, *Toute Allure* and *Tout Soul*

'An amusing and well-observed romp through the brocantes of south-west France inhabited by a host of colourful characters – a must for lovers of all things French. Lovejoy for Francophiles!'

Marc Allum, antiques specialist on the *Antiques Roadshow*

'A brilliant evocation of the life of French brocanteurs, full of camaraderie and incident, just make sure the woodu   -   do.'

Ja

Praise for *Serge Bastarde Ate My Baguette*:

'*Dummer describes a very different France... Bastarde
certainly lives up to his surname, cruising the countryside
in his battered van tying to cheat clueless peasants
out of their heirlooms. But Bastarde grows on you,
with his imaginative lies and unexpected generosity.*'

THE FINANCIAL TIMES

'*Get a copy. You'll love it.*'

ANTIQUES DIARY

'*The book's startling title [is] surely up there as
one of the best of the year... amusing... a nicely
observed insight into rural life in south-west
France. For the price, it's a bargain (hunt).*

FRENCH Magazine

'*Well written and set at an engaging pace, this comic
autobiographical narrative wends its way through the
daily lives of the author and his ex-pat community, as
well as the day-to-day events of the local inhabitants
of the area... this easy-to-read humorous account of
one man's expat dream turning into an all-too-harsh
reality is an enjoyable read. Filled with eccentric
characters and unlikely adventures, this is a highly
amusing romp through the real rural France.*'

LIVING FRANCE

John Dummer

SON

~of~

SERGE BASTARDE

MAYHEM *in the*
ANTIQUES MARKETS
of RURAL FRANCE

SON OF SERGE BASTARDE

Copyright © John Dummer, 2012

Summersdale Publishers Ltd
46 West Street
Chichester
West Sussex
PO19 1RP
UK

www.summersdale.com

Printed and bound by CPI Group (UK) Ltd, Croydon

ISBN: 978-1-84953-150-4

Substantial discounts on bulk quantities of Summersdale books are available to corporations, professional associations and other organisations. For details telephone Summersdale Publishers on (+44-1243-771107), fax (+44-1243-786300) or email (nicky@summersdale.com).

For my darling Helen

Photo by my wife Helen

ABOUT THE AUTHOR

John Dummer has worked as a reporter on a local paper, a music business press officer, a record plugger and a broadcaster. As a drummer in the 1960s he toured with his own John Dummer Blues Band, had a number one hit in France, 'Nine By Nine', and toured with legendary blues acts like Howlin' Wolf, John Lee Hooker and Lowell Fulson. In the 1970s he drummed with the hit doo-wop revival group Darts and met his wife Helen when she was the photographer on a Darts photo session. After Darts John and Helen formed their own group, True Life Confessions, and had a top fifty hit with their version of 'Blues Skies'. John went on to manage the powerhouse rock trio The Screaming Blue Messiahs and after three years of touring the States, burned out from all the madness, he upped sticks with Helen and moved to France. There followed a two-year sojourn living in a windmill in the Alentejo region of Portugal, and a return to France with finances much depleted. They discovered if they registered as *brocanteurs* (antiques dealers) they could work and be covered under the excellent French health system. It was working in the French outdoor antiques markets and the amusing and fascinating characters he met that inspired John to write his first book, *Serge Bastarde Ate My Baguette*. John and Helen now live in south-west France in the middle of the Landes forest with their dog Buster and quite a lot of cats.

CONTENTS

PREFACE

A few years ago my wife Helen and I bought a 300-year-old farmhouse in need of restoration in the Chalosse region of the Landes in France. We had always dabbled in antiques in England and discovered that if we registered as *brocanteurs* we could hopefully earn an income working in the colourful outdoor markets in south-west France and be covered under their excellent health system. But we had to learn about French antiques from scratch and needed help.

My mentor appeared in the form of a short, tough Frenchman with wiry grey hair and a ready wit. His name: Serge Bastarde. When he found out I was English he went out of his way to be helpful and took it upon himself to show me the ropes. He invited me to accompany him on his trips out in the country to 'forage for hidden treasures'. I soon discovered he was a bit of a rogue but he gradually won me over and we became firm friends.

A couple of years into our friendship Serge romanced and fell in love with another dealer's wife, Angelique, and much to our surprise they ran off together to Martinique. Helen and Angelique had become friends and kept in touch, but after a while the emails and phone calls stopped. We had no idea how to get in contact with them or where they were. What had happened to Serge Bastarde? It was a mystery...

1

BLUE BEAT AND LITTLE MONKEYS

'Oh, fish knives and chintzy tea sets? Now there's a novelty, what!'

A snooty-faced bloke sporting a ponytail and wearing a deerstalker hat and plus fours loomed over my stand. 'Every time I come past you're selling some tat. It's extremely galling.' He pulled a supercilious face, and picked up a cup and saucer from my table to examine them.

'Eugh! Country Roses, how tasteless. I used to sell this sort of rubbish when I first started doing the markets here. So common.'

'The French seem to like them,' I said. 'I sell quite a few.'

'Yes, well they don't know any better.' And with that he turned on his heel and strode off.

From his exaggerated toffee-nosed manner and upper-class accent he could only be English. But the deerstalker and plus fours? He was like a P. G. Wodehouse character come to life. I watched open-mouthed as he disappeared into the crowd, his grey ponytail bobbing. Amazing! He couldn't possibly be for real.

I was at a fair in the square of a little village called Soumoulou on the road from Pau to Tarbes, not far from Lourdes. The market is held right through the year and takes place on the first Sunday of each month. In the distance, the blue-grey mountains of the Pyrenees were silhouetted against the skyline. So far it had gone well. I had been selling since I opened at eight-thirty that morning.

I couldn't help feeling a bit put out, though, after suffering the snooty bloke's criticism. I had regular, loyal customers who just wanted chintzy tea sets, after all. It amused them, they assured me, to serve up tea and cakes 'comme les Anglais' (English-style) to their friends. The French enjoy reminding us that we English love tea, and they find our obsession with it charming and slightly quaint.

I was contemplating a quick visit to the cafe when my attention was caught by a customer. She was interested in a polished mahogany Davenport that my wife Helen had picked up in England on one of our trips over there to buy stock. I explained how the diminutive desk was light and easily transportable. She was enchanted but appeared slightly put off by the price, even though it was, in my estimation, quite reasonable. During my time working the antique markets in France I had found that the French public in general were sometimes unaware of the value of desirable pieces of English furniture, although with changes in fashion they were learning fast. The woman said she liked the desk but wanted to fetch her husband to look at it.

A few French dealers had turned up early looking for a bargain and now the Spanish dealers were beginning to arrive with wallets stuffed full of euros. They liked mahogany in Spain and I was hoping to sell the Davenport for a good price.

I recognised a pair of Spanish dealers. One was a whey-faced, hugely overweight chain-smoker who wore dazzling white trainers and always carried a black silver-topped cane. His companion was short, dark and animated, with a warm, friendly manner. They were examining the antique wooden boxes I had placed in a prominent position on our black-cloth-covered tables. It is only the English and sometimes the Dutch who use black covers on their stands. The French find black far too funereal, preferring a clean white sheet. Louis, my French dealer friend who shares my love of jazz and blues, had recently pointed this out to me.

'All that black – it looks like you should have a corpse on your table, or a bunch of chrysanthemums,' he chuckled.

We had made that mistake with the chrysanthemums when we first moved to France. Invited to dinner by neighbours we brought them a lovely pot of chrysanths, only to be greeted by a look of abject horror. We discovered later that these flowers are only ever used to decorate graves on All Saints' Eve (Halloween) – you would never give chrysanths to a living person.

The big fat Spaniard with the silver-topped cane smiled and beckoned me over. He spoke French falteringly, or as the expression has it, 'comme une vache espagnole' (like a Spanish cow). He held up one of the boxes and grinned good-naturedly.

'How much for all of these?' he asked, indicating three beautifully crafted Edwardian mahogany boxes. One was a writing slope and the other two had originally been tea caddies but had been altered to hold jewellery or other precious objects. This always threw me – having to work out a deal on several items. Maths was never my strong point, and I sometimes made awful mistakes under pressure. When I was a lad my dad decided to coach me in arithmetic and had the misguided belief that clipping me round the back of the head when I made a mistake would help me to learn. This traumatised me and had the opposite effect, putting me off numbers for life. My wife Helen, though, has always been understanding and had recently bought me a small calculator, which I actually felt too embarrassed to use in front of other dealers. My method in this instance was to jot down the prices, add them up, and then try to work out a reasonable discount. As they were regular customers I would try to give them a decent reduction. Spanish dealers appreciate this, and if you give them a good deal they come back again and again.

I told the chubby dealer how much and he immediately said in English, 'Best price... last price?' These were handy bartering phrases he had learnt from trips to England buying in the big fairs at Ardingly and Newark. I knocked off another fifty euros and there were smiles all round. I had obviously made a mistake and been overgenerous. In their expensive antiques shop in Spain they were going to treble or quadruple what they had paid me. I bubble-wrapped and slid the boxes into plastic bags and they went off happy, clutching their bargain purchases.

As I watched them go a small child in red dungarees came tottering past my stand. He must have only been about three years old. He looked up, caught my eye and smiled. I'm a sucker for kids. I gave him a little wave and a grin. He stood unsteadily for a moment and then teetered towards me, grabbing at the side of one of my tables. I rushed forward, worried he would pull the covers and send my stock flying and injure himself in the process, but he stopped as if hypnotised. He had spotted my little clockwork antique toy monkey. He had good taste, I'll give him that. The monkey was furry and when you wound him up he hopped about and banged a pair of cymbals together. He was a favourite of mine, an original tin toy manufactured in the 1950s by the Japanese company Daishin. I was secretly in no hurry to sell him. The child reached up and grasped it, bringing it up close to his face. He examined it carefully and suddenly put it in his mouth. I rushed forward again as I felt it was neither hygienic nor good for a valuable toy to be put in a child's mouth. But he saw me coming, gave me a mischievous look and ran away gleefully, clutching the monkey in his grubby little hands.

I couldn't believe it! I looked around. How come this young child was wandering about unaccompanied? It didn't make sense. And he'd got my monkey!

I nipped round my tables and went after him. He was only a toddler; he couldn't have gone far. But when I looked up the aisles, hoping to spot his red dungarees, there was no sign of him. He seemed to have vanished into thin air. I ran from stand to stand asking if anyone had seen a small child holding a toy monkey. Thibaut, a young rugby-playing furniture dealer friend of mine, said, 'He went that way, John,' pointing towards the other stands. And looking across the aisles I caught a glimpse of red and ran towards it. But when I got to where I thought he was, there was no sign of him. Things were turning a bit surreal – it was as if I had suddenly become an extra in the film *Don't Look Now* (the one where Donald Sutherland keeps seeing a little child in a red mac) and I was beginning to worry about my stand. Leaving it unattended like this was asking for trouble. I ran around frantically, looking under tables, trying to catch sight of him, but there were too many people milling about.

I gave up and headed back and it was just as well I did because the woman who had been looking at the Davenport desk earlier had returned with her husband and they were examining it together. I was still thinking about my lost monkey and, although it was a good sign that the woman had brought her husband, I wasn't too optimistic. In my experience, husbands are usually less than enamoured of items their wives want to purchase. I'm just the same when Helen wants to buy something. I'm often underwhelmed. It's the thought of parting with money that causes the male of the species to frown and look disinterested. I waited, fully expecting the husband to put her off. But on the contrary, he seemed as charmed by the desk as she was. My hopes rose as they actually looked like they might buy it. The woman wanted to know a bit more about it. The French love to discuss the provenance and history of an antique. I was about to explain how this was an unusual and desirable piece when I was rudely interrupted. The stuck-up bloke with the ponytail and deerstalker suddenly reappeared and began to hold forth in a loud, haughty voice.

'C'est un Davenport, Madame. C'est très, très populaire en Angleterre!'

He made no attempt at a French accent. He just sounded like a self-satisfied English snob speaking a foreign language in a loud voice.

The French couple looked bemused. Who was this strange man? They smiled politely but I could see from their expressions that he was putting them off.

'Mais oui, le premier était attribué à Captain Davenport, un Anglais dans l'armée.'

What was he going on about? I felt like telling him to bugger off. This upper-class twit coupled with the loss of my monkey had put me in a bad mood. Under my breath, through clenched teeth, I muttered, 'Don't help me!'

I smiled at the couple, embarrassed. They weren't sure if this was a set-up and he was working with me to pressurise them into buying the desk. The idiot was totally thick-skinned. He began to pull out the little side drawers and explain how useful they were. Then he showed them how the desk could be moved around on its small brass castors. I tried to make light of his bombastic behaviour and take over, but it was obvious the couple had had enough. They made an excuse and said they were going off to think about it. I watched them walk away, fuming at how he had ruined my sale.

But he was oblivious. He picked up an old ukulele from my table and began plunking at it. The smug bastard was pleased with himself! He began singing 'When I'm cleaning winders, when I'm cleaning winders!' tunelessly in a high-pitched voice like George Formby.

'These things never sell,' he said. 'Can't give 'em away.'

He dumped the ukulele on the table and ambled off, still singing to himself.

The swine! I wanted to run after him and hit him on the head with the instrument. If I whipped off his deerstalker and bonked him one, I could probably knock the git out!

I was still seething when Reg, an English dealer I knew well, wandered past. Reg was a tattooed rough diamond and an unlikely antiques dealer. He had worked the French markets for years and was also quite scary, but a 'salt-of-the-earth' bloke who would help you out if you were in trouble. Rumour had it he'd 'done time' in French and Spanish prisons for various drug-related offences. He and his rangy and wild wife, Rita, complemented each other perfectly. They regularly stalled out at the *brocante* markets. I asked him if he knew the ponytailed pain with the deerstalker and plus fours.

'Oh, you mean Lord Snooty?'

'Lord Snooty? Is that his name?'

'Nah, I just call him that. His real name is Algie.'

'Algie?' I was taken aback. 'I've never met anyone called Algie in my life.'

'Well, I say that,' continued Reg, 'but his actual name is Colin. He just tells everyone his name is Algie. I found a wallet once. No money in it so I looked at the passport and it said Colin Baxter, with Snooty's photo in it. I got the organisers to announce it over the loudspeakers and saw him slope off to collect it, embarrassed as everyone knows him as Algie. He's a right snob... well, fake. I can't stand people like that but it's good for a laugh. I enjoy taking the mickey out of him.'

'I don't find him at all funny,' I said, and explained how he'd blown my sale.

'Yeah, well he's a right Francophile. He hates all the expats over here, even if he does play the Hooray Henry Englishman to the hilt. The French love him for it. He treats me like dirt and the feeling's mutual. He gets right up my nose. Take no notice of him. Insult him if he gets on yer nerves. I call him a wanker and tell him to piss off. He can't do much about it.'

I thanked Reg for the advice and said I'd do the same next time Algie or Colin, or whatever his name was, came round and tried to mess up one of my sales again. I asked Reg if he'd seen a small child in red dungarees and told him how he'd stolen my monkey.

'Now you come to mention it, I saw that kid earlier. He's a tough little bruiser. I had to shoo him away. He was trying to touch stuff on my stand.'

'You don't know who his parents are? Only I was kind of hoping to get my monkey back.'

'I'm not sure but I think he belongs to one of the *brocanteurs*.'

'You don't know which one exactly?'

'He was with a young bloke I haven't seen before. He's stalled out round the back somewhere.'

I thanked him and headed back to my stand, deciding to have a walk around later when it was quieter and try to find the child. It had turned into a bright sunny morning and the market was packed with people in a buying mood. I was so busy I almost forgot about my monkey and Lord Snooty and his interfering ways.

Before I knew it, it was midday and I was beginning to feel hungry, ready to grab a quick lunch. I knew the dealer next to me. She was a kindly woman named Chantal. I had often watched her stand for her when she made her rounds visiting her friends on the market, getting all the latest gossip. I stowed away some of my more valuable items and indicated to her that I was off for a bite to eat and asked if she could keep an eye on my stand for me. She smiled and gave me a wink. My gear was safe in her hands. She would watch anyone looking at my stuff like a hawk, drive a hard bargain on a sale and keep any money safe for me.

As I crossed the square I noticed other dealers heading for the cafe. I passed a battered shooting brake with a trailer on the back. One of the side doors was open and the car sound system was pumping out loud music. I stopped and listened because I recognised the track. It was quite an obscure one – 'Take Me Home Country Roads' by Toots and the Maytals. Fantastic! This segued into Toots' original version of 'Monkey Man' followed by Jimmy James and the Vagabonds' early blue-beat version of the Neil Diamond song 'Red, Red Wine' – three of my all-time favourites. I hadn't heard them for years. I was surprised to see Lord Snooty appear round the back of the trailer carrying a large framed oil painting which he hung up on a wooden stand. I couldn't believe my eyes or ears. Did he have good musical taste? It seemed unlikely.

I couldn't help myself. I smiled and shouted across to him, 'Jimmy James and the Vagabonds – I used to see them at the Marquee in the sixties. Great band!'

He leant over and turned down the sound. 'The Marquee? I was always down the Marquee,' he said. 'And the Roaring Twenties, and the Flamingo.'

'The Flamingo All-niter, what! Georgie Fame and the Blue Flames, Herbie Goins and the Nightimers, Zoot Money and the Big Roll Band... those were the days,' I said. Way before I turned to antique dealing I'd had a colourful history in the music industry, writing a weekly pop column, then working for CBS Records, and later forming the John Dummer Blues Band, which toured Britain and Europe during the blues boom of the sixties. Hearing those tunes really took me back.

He extended his hand and we shook. 'Name's Algie. Always pleased to meet anyone who spent their youth down the Marquee and the Flamingo. Did you manage to sell that Davenport?'

'No, thanks to you,' I said sarcastically.

'Ah yes, those certainly were the days,' he said, ignoring my remark.

'We must have been down the same clubs together,' I said. And then, before I knew what I was saying, it just came out: 'Fancy a drink over the caff?'

'Oh yah, certainly,' he replied. 'I'll just cover up and join you.'

I wished I hadn't been so hasty. What was I thinking, inviting this twat for coffee? But he did have great taste in music – I had to give him that.

'How has your morning been?' I asked.

'Absolute rubbish. I haven't even broken even. I hope this afternoon is better or I might just have to top myself.'

'That bad, eh?' I couldn't help myself. I was secretly glad he'd lost money.

'I used to sell crap like yours when I started doing the markets here,' he said. 'But I got sick of all that.'

I bet you did, I thought to myself, *you belittling pain. Maybe you should go back to it if it was more successful.*

'You sell paintings now, do you?' I said, indicating the framed oil he had just put on display. It was horrendous; one of the worst examples of modern art I'd ever seen. A monkey could have done better.

'Quality works of art, yes,' he said, 'and good French bronzes when I can get hold of them. I much prefer to handle tasteful antiques.'

He shut his trailer and we headed off across the square. I was hoping I wasn't going to regret this. I still wasn't over the loss of my monkey or the pantomime with the Davenport. If he started acting up, giving himself airs or playing the silly goat again, I wasn't sure how I'd react. But looking at him now with his deerstalker and plus fours and his stuck-up manner I couldn't stop smiling to myself. Colin, Algie or Lord Snooty? He was so over the top he was comical.

2

GOLD, CASH AND QUESTIONS

The cafe was packed with dealers grabbing a quick drink and a bite to eat. Thibaut walked over, lager in hand, and offered to buy me a beer.

'Thanks,' I said, 'but I'd prefer a Coke.' He'd forgotten I was a reformed alcoholic sworn off the booze. It was often hard work to convince the French that I was teetotal. They really have no concept of what that means. It's almost as bad as being a vegetarian, which is totally unfathomable to them.

'Did you get your monkey back?' he asked, chuckling. I told him I couldn't find the little blighter who took it but I wasn't giving up hope. I knew Thibaut liked a jolly good laugh. The pair of us had hung out with our mutual friend Serge Bastarde before he had set off for pastures new, and our talk as ever turned to Serge and the laughs we had as we reminisced about old times.

'Do you remember the first time you saw Angelique?' asked Thibaut. 'Before Serge stole her from that *gars terrible* [awful guy], Bernard. Serge and I knew she was prone to stripping off in public but you had no idea. That's why we hung around waiting for her to disrobe, but your face was priceless and you were so shocked when she started modelling those corsets she and Bernard were selling.'

'You're right, I couldn't believe it,' I said. 'But we were all even more amazed when she fell for Serge and they went off to live in Martinique. You don't have any news of them, do you?'

'I heard they had a baby about three years ago,' said Thibaut, 'but since then nothing... *disparu.*'

Lord Snooty butted in. 'Did I hear you right? You're not talking about that frightful oik Serge Bastarde, are you? An absolute bounder.' He looked appalled.

'He wasn't that bad,' I said. 'We are friends of his.'

'Well, you've got no taste, then. He's the most awful little man – you're well rid of him. We English have to represent our country like ambassadors, but Serge Bastarde displays all the worst traits of the French – greedy, money-grabbing and crooked, the lot of 'em.'

I stood open-mouthed. Reg had said Algie was a Francophile, but this pontificating was the racist diatribe of a complete ignoramus. And he wasn't about to stop.

'They're double-dealers in business, all their politicians get away with murder, they think they're great lovers but they have no idea how to treat a woman – unlike us Brits – their bureaucracy is a farce, and they guillotined all their superiors and betters and let the rabble and peasants take over.'

I could see that Thibaut was starting to look annoyed. Lord Snooty was obviously rubbing him up the wrong way, and although Thibaut was usually quite easygoing, when riled he was a man you'd want to avoid.

Lord Snooty (or Algie, or whatever), oblivious to the glowering Thibaut, carried on denigrating Serge and the French until he finished with: 'I'd say that most of the French are thieves and liars like Serge and that he's the type that gives us *brocanteurs* a bad name.'

Thibaut exploded and lurched forward. He'd had enough. He grabbed Algie by the front of his jacket and lifted him bodily off the ground, cursing him nose to nose with some pretty strong swear words, several of which I hadn't heard before. He called him an English *rosbif* snob and let go, dropping him so he staggered and fell backwards.

'I'm sorry, John,' said Thibaut, 'but I can't stay around listening to this *connard* any longer. I won't be responsible for my actions.' He took a final swig of his lager and walked out.

Algie was dusting himself down. 'I don't much care for the company you keep,' he said to me. 'Are all your friends absolute blackguards like him and that Bastarde fellow?'

I told him in no uncertain terms that I disagreed strongly with everything he'd said and that he'd gone too far. I walked out, furious. Outside I made a spurt to catch up with Thibaut.

'I'm sorry about all that, Thibaut,' I said. 'I've only just met the bloke. I don't know him at all. He gives all us English a bad name. We aren't all rude like that, it's really embarrassing.'

'*C'est pas grave*,' said Thibaut (it doesn't matter). 'I know Serge was no angel, but he is one of us – we must stick together.'

I wished him luck and *bon courage* and made my way back to my stand. Amazing! Serge was still causing me trouble when he wasn't even in the same country.

Surprisingly enough, Chantal had sold a silver-plated tea set for the full price on the ticket and she handed me the money in euro notes. I thanked her from the bottom of my heart and asked if she could watch my pitch a bit longer. I was determined to track down that toddler, the one who stole my monkey.

I set off, checking every stand I passed. Most of the dealers were back from lunch and I was obliged to stop and greet everyone and have a chat. Fred, a book dealer I knew well, said he had seen the child in the red dungarees and pointed me towards a stand further along.

I looked across, and sure enough there was the kid, sitting in a little chair out front. He saw me coming and I don't know if he recognised me but he got up and sidled round behind the legs of the young dealer running the stand. I had never seen this young *brocanteur* before and was surprised to see he was wearing – somewhat inappropriately for a *brocante* fair – white hip-hop gear set off with a touch of 'bling': a glittering gold neck chain, sparkling ear studs and a flashy watch. I smiled at him and bent down and looked at the kid.

'He's a lad, isn't he?' I said, laughing. 'How old is he?'

The guy looked at me with a surly expression.

'He's not a boy, he's a girl.' He pulled a face that implied he thought I was a complete imbecile for making such an obviously stupid mistake.

'Oh yes, of course, sorry,' I said. I now noticed the little sparkling studs in the child's ears. The Spanish and some French are in the habit of having their baby girls' ears pierced. But, as Reg said, this kid was a tough little bruiser – bit of an easy mistake to make in this case.

As I stood up I noticed my little monkey sitting on one of his tables. It had a ticket on it and it was up for sale. I was speechless.

I stuttered in disbelief, *'Ce petit singe, il vient d'où?'* (The little monkey, where did you get him?)

The young dealer sneered and shrugged like he couldn't understand me.

I explained in the nicest possible way that the little girl had taken it off my stand to play with earlier and that the monkey belonged to me.

The guy blanked me and made a dismissive gesture. He turned his back. He wasn't the slightest bit interested.

I could see I wasn't getting anywhere and was determined not to lose my monkey so I decided to find the market organiser to get him to sort it out. The man who ran the

Soumoulou market was an impressive bearded individual who stood no nonsense from anyone. We arrived back at the young dealer's stand together and as soon as he saw the organiser his whole attitude changed. Faced with the pair of us he explained that the little girl had come back with the monkey and he thought she had found it thrown away somewhere or been given it as a gift. He was unaware it belonged to me, he pleaded. I couldn't do anything other than accept his profuse apologies, take my monkey and return to my stand, vindicated.

It had been a somewhat unsettling day but in the end I had done OK and made a decent profit. By late afternoon most of the customers had drifted off and I began to pack up. Someone had left a couple of flyers on my stand. I threw them in my rubbish bag without giving them a second glance and continued packing. As I was taking down my parasol I noticed another leaflet stuck to my shoe. There were a few of them strewn around the place. I stopped and pulled it off. It was a flyer boasting the offer 'ACHAT D'OR'. There was a photo of a character smiling enticingly and holding up a wad of euro notes. He looked very familiar. When I looked more closely... I couldn't believe my eyes.

I heard a distinctive voice and looked up to see Lord Snooty coming towards me, jubilantly waving one of the same leaflets in his hand.

'There, what did I tell you? Isn't this your pal Serge Bastarde?' He was pointing at the photo triumphantly.

SON OF SERGE BASTARDE

'Now tell me the chap's not an oik and a bounder. Serge the Snurge! I rest my case.'

Yes, the smug prig was right. I now knew without a doubt it really was true. My eyes weren't deceiving me. It was Serge, as large as life. I'd recognise that face anywhere. And the way he was fanning the ever familiar fistful of euros – Serge Bastarde, in all his glory, plying the old cash-for-gold scam.

What the hell was he playing at and where the hell was he?

And if he was back, why the hell hadn't he got in touch with me?

3

SWALLOWS AND FIELDS OF CORN

The maize in the fields that surround our house was ripe and rustling in the morning sunshine. The russet pods that protected the corn had peeled back in places to reveal glimpses of the shiny yellow ears enveloped by silky spun cushions. The stalks of corn were now fully grown and we were completely hidden from the outside world. I loved early autumn, when the corn was at its highest and it felt like we were in a little secret world of our own.

In the distance I could clearly see the shadowy blue outline of the Pyrenees. When the mountains are visible in this area of the Landes, it means that rain is coming within the next couple of days. Our neighbours had told us this when we first arrived here and at first we had been dubious. It sounded like an old wives' tale to us but they were right. It doesn't matter how fine it is or how brightly the sun is shining; if you can see the Pyrenees, rain is on its way.

The fields of corn owned by Mr Fagot sloped gently down to Mr Leglise's farm and that morning I could hear his dog's excited barking and his yells of encouragement as the spry octogenarian drove his donkey and cow out into the pasture for the day. This meant it was eight o'clock; you could set your watch by the time Mr Leglise drove his livestock out into the fields.

What a perfect morning for a stroll into the village to buy fresh croissants for breakfast! I told Helen where I was going and set off along the track across the fields. I had showed her the 'ACHAT D'OR' leaflet but she didn't believe it; she said someone must have used an old photo of Serge. I tried not to think about it. Instead, I did what I always do when I walk across my land – worry about the weeds and brambles that take hold over the summer. And then guilt sets in as I recall the ecological disaster I caused through my ignorance when we first moved into our 300-year-old farmhouse a few years ago. There was a jungle of weeds round the house and one of our well-meaning French neighbours had advised me to control them with a chlorate weedkiller. I bought a plastic pump machine, diluted the concentrated killer and went around spraying the paths and driveway, wearing a face mask and goggles (you can't be too careful with poisonous weedkiller, it said on the bottle with its skull-and-crossbones logo).

It worked like magic. After a few days the weeds wilted and died and the effect lasted throughout the year. I was so encouraged by this that the following season I went right round the house spraying the bottom of the walls where the weeds were springing up. And I noticed I wasn't the only one caught up in this weed-killing mania. Our neighbours sprayed the verges outside their houses, leaving just a dead area of earth where nothing could grow, not even grass. This had seemed a bit extreme, but as the French like to point out, *'C'est propre'* (It's neat).

On hot, humid summer evenings we were delighted to hear the sweet musical peeping sounds made by tiny green tree frogs around our house. Sometimes we would see one attached to one of the windows by the sucker pads on its feet. They were such wonderful little frogs, and the sound they made was magical. But the following summer they had disappeared, and with horror we realised too late that our beautiful tree frogs must have absorbed the deadly weedkiller. I had thoughtlessly wiped out a population that had doubtlessly been breeding round our property for generations. We hoped and prayed that some had survived and they would return. But they never did.

The EU has recently banned chlorate weedkiller, and not before time. Now I never use weedkiller – I cut back the brambles and weeds by hand. This is not as effective and is much harder work, but I will never be able to rid myself of the guilt over the demise of our beautiful tree-frog colony.

As I walked through the orchard behind our house the church bell in the village chimed quarter past the hour and I remembered Spike, our big brindle Staffordshire bull terrier who was buried in the far corner of the field. A walk without a dog isn't the same, and with Spike by my side the world had always seemed a brighter and more exciting place. He had a unique, stylish way of trotting that you couldn't help but admire, and his whole mien was the epitome of relaxed and casual 'cool'. This was the first time Helen and I had been without a Staff since we were first married. We had brought two cats with us and inherited two more from Gaston, the previous owner of the house, but to my mind there's something about having a dog around that makes life more worthwhile. I can think back to every dog I've ever had and how each one enriched my life. My earliest memories are of cuddling up in a basket with Bruce, a gentle red setter that befriended me on a beach in Worthing when I was a kid on holiday with my mum and dad. Bruce's owners were unable to cope with him for some reason and to my great joy agreed to let us keep him. As I grew up we had a succession of black Labradors and I still miss my little whippet-cross, Percy, my constant companion in my early twenties.

We had spent too long without having a dog around. I decided when I got back with the croissants I would talk to Helen over breakfast about buying a Staff puppy. There must be a breeder here in France. American Staffs had become popular in recent years, although they were on the dangerous dogs list in France. But the Staffordshire bull terrier had been removed from 'list 2' after protests by owners in France, so now you didn't have to register the dogs with the local *mairie* (town hall), or muzzle them, or get special insurance.

As I followed the road into our village the *hirondelles* (swallows) were swooping low, gliding effortlessly over the fields. It wouldn't be long before they would begin to gather on the telephone lines in preparation for their migration before the cooler weather arrived. When we had first moved into this house years ago it was the beginning of summer and a pair of swallows flew in through the back door and all around the living room, twittering, landing on the beam above the *cheminée* (fireplace) and back out of the door. It was thrilling having them whirl about indoors above our heads. When we examined the beam we discovered an old nest hidden underneath it. The previous owner, Gaston, must have left the back door open all summer long and the pair were returning to lay eggs and raise chicks in the same nest. There were several cats prowling around and the swallows sensibly decided it was too risky and, to our disappointment, went off to nest elsewhere.

Seeing the swallows flying reminded me of the old French song I learnt when I was a child, 'Alouette, Gentille Alouette'. The *alouette* is not a swallow but a skylark, and it was only recently that I discovered the song was about plucking the feathers from the corpse of the bird before eating it. Somehow this took away the magic for me, although it is still a pretty tune.

On the way back from the *boulangerie* with my croissants I bumped into Roland, a woodcutter and farmer who lives nearby. In his spare time he plays accordion and sings in a local dance band that plays at fetes and *bals à papa* (old-fashioned traditional dances). He knows I'm a musician too and we had hit it off as soon as we met.

'Heh, John, it's going to liven things up when they build the houses on the fields next to your place,' he grinned. 'We could do with some new blood round here.'

'How do you mean?' I said. I didn't know what he was talking about.

'*Mais oui*, they've changed the law. We farmers can sell off our fields for building land. They've extended the limits of the village. There's been a notice up in the *mairie* for months.'

My heart sank. We'd heard nothing about this and never went to the *mairie* to read the notices.

'Old man Fagot has applied for permission to build on his fields next to your place. I saw him in the bar last night and he was rubbing his hands together. He's going to make a fortune.'

'What? He's going to build houses on the fields next to us?' I couldn't believe what I was hearing.

'All us farmers want to sell if we can. There's no money in farming now. We have our old age to consider.'

I was stunned. Surely this wasn't happening. We had been told that if we were surrounded by farmland we were protected here in France. The law was that agricultural land was safe from development. I had been enjoying the peace and serenity of fields of corn around our house. If they built on them, it would all vanish. I felt my knees go weak.

'Isn't there anything we can do to stop it?' I asked.

'Stop it?' Roland seemed surprised. 'Why would you want to stop it? You'll have lots more new friends and neighbours. It will do wonders for the village. We need the money that it will bring for developing better amenities – it will mean bigger fetes and more work for our dance band, not to mention all the pretty young girls.' He gave me a nudge and a wink. Roland was something of a local Lothario. He lived with his eighty-year-old mother but still kept in touch with a brace of ex-wives he continued to visit and spoon with. He also wasn't averse to taking up with any new girlfriends who might pass his way – the younger and prettier the better. He clearly viewed any enlargement of the neighbourhood as a chance for new fodder to enliven his sex life.

I looked at him in a state of shock, bid him a hurried *'au revoir'* and half walked, half ran back up the road. My heart was thumping. Could it be true? All these beautiful fields to be concreted over to build new houses? What would that mean for us? We loved the away-from-it-all rural atmosphere of our place.

As I passed Mr Leglise's he was scything the long grass in front of his old stone farmhouse dressed in traditional French blue jacket and trousers, his beret set at a jaunty angle. He would be affected by the new houses, too. I went up to him but he was so engrossed he didn't notice me and I had to jump back to avoid being cut down by his scythe. He grinned at me in apology, put down the tool and shook my hand.

'Have you heard the news?' I asked him. 'Fagot is selling off his fields to build houses.'

'Yes, I know,' he said, 'but there's not much we can do about it now, he's made up his mind.'

'You knew about this?' I was shocked. Everyone seemed to know but us.

'I could have sold some of my land but I don't think new neighbours would put up with my singing, do you?' he said. On sunny days he was in the habit of getting out his old gramophone, playing records and singing along to them in his rich baritone voice. 'What about your drumming, John? I love it when you practise but not everyone likes the sound of drums like I do. You might have problems, too.'

I didn't know what to say. Everything was about to change round here. I bid him a hurried goodbye and headed home.

When I arrived, breathless and stressed out, Helen was waiting to have breakfast with me. I blurted it out: 'They're going to plough up the fields and build a load of houses! What are we going to do?'

'What are you talking about?' She was pouring herself a cup of tea.

'I just saw Roland. He says they've changed the law in France and farmers can sell off their land for building plots.'

Helen looked at me like I had gone mad. 'That's impossible! They're not allowed to.'

'They are, and they have. He says Fagot's selling his and they're going to build houses on his fields. Roland says there's a meeting at the town hall next week when they're going to give the details to everyone.'

Helen looked at me, wide-eyed. 'No, that can't be true?'

'Roland seemed very definite about it,' I said. 'Mr Leglise knows all about it as well.'

'I can't believe it,' she exploded. 'I'm going up to the *mairie* to ask what's going on.' She leapt up, grabbed the car keys and ran out.

I sat and waited, gazing across at the heady countryside surrounding our peaceful old *mas*, listlessly munching on a croissant. But now it had somehow lost its taste. I mused over the path that had brought us to live in this old house together. I had met Helen whilst I was playing in the band Darts, formed some years after the John Dummer Blues Band disbanded. She was a photographer on a band shoot and I fell madly in love with her and we got married. Some years later, after touring and managing other music ventures, I realised I was disenchanted with the music business and burnt out. Helen and I were both fond of France, and it was at this point that we decided, on a whim, to buy an ancient monastery in the Dordogne. We lived there for a couple of years before selling up and touring around Europe, finally settling in Portugal, where we found an old windmill on a hill in the Alentejo region. We lived 'wild and free' before returning to France with finances much depleted and had bought the 300-year-old farmhouse, which was then in need of much restoration.

When Helen got back twenty minutes later she looked desperate.

'They're building a housing estate next to us!'

'What?'

'Not just a few houses on the road but a whole *lotissement*.'

She was clutching photocopies of the plans and we pored over them in disbelief. The new *zone constructible* (building zone) covered the area around our house and included our garden and fields.

'They said we could build two houses on our land if we wanted to,' she said. 'Apparently the law changed in the whole of France recently and all villages are allowed to apply to enlarge the building zones around them. Fagot has permission to build a twenty-house *lotissement* right next to us.'

'Twenty houses? The whole of France?' I'd gone gaga. 'Why didn't we know about it? How come the neighbours weren't all talking about it?'

'I don't know, do I?' said Helen, sounding irritated. 'I stopped at the neighbours' on the road opposite us and they had no idea what I was talking about. They're beside themselves now that I've told them they're going to have twenty houses across the way. They were going straight up the *mairie* when I left them. I suppose people who wanted to sell and build kept it quiet. How often does anyone read notices up the *mairie*?'

'Can't we fight them?' I asked.

'I don't think so, not according to the mayor – he's ecstatic! I think we're going to have to move,' said Helen.

'What? I don't want to move. I love it here,' I said, feeling like I was about to burst into tears.

'Well, you can stay if you want,' said Helen, 'but I'm going.'

Now the truth was out! She had been trying to persuade me to move for ages but I had dug my heels in. She wasn't as enamoured of the bathtub in the kitchen as I was. She kept saying we should face up to the fact that restoring a house wasn't our forte and it had beaten us. I had rerooted it with the help of an English builder friend and rewired most of the house, but never got round to installing a proper kitchen or bathroom. Maybe she was right. We might as well move and start afresh.

The following Wednesday evening we were sitting in the *halle des sports* (sports hall) with everyone else in the village, listening to the mayor telling us about plans for the future. Any protest should have been lodged with the *mairie* months ago. We got the feeling there had been some sleight of hand somewhere along the line and that there were very few objectors. Everyone seemed just to accept it – except us. No one else said anything. Our house appeared to be the only one encompassed by a *lotissement*; all the others were on the edge of the road. Looking at a map it appeared that the *zone constructible* had been specifically extended out in a big loop to the edge of our property to take in all the fields around us. And the twenty houses had been an underestimation; Fagot envisioned over forty plots being sold off, with new houses encircling our home completely.

We came away feeling depressed and defeated. But I still wasn't willing to give up.

'We could plant some tall leylandii trees to grow up along the boundary of our land to hide us from the estate,' I suggested, clutching at straws. 'How bad could it be?'

'I really don't know, but I'm not staying to find out,' said Helen with feeling.

4

BUYING FRENZY

It was still dark as I drove into Dax, but the town was slowly beginning to come to life. It was a warm, balmy morning and the colourful neon signs outside the numerous *boulangeries* gave the town a jolly party atmosphere. I like the way French bakers begin work at an astonishingly early hour and that you can purchase freshly baked bread or croissants before sunup. This is a blessing, especially on Saturday or Sunday mornings when revellers and wedding guests are wending their weary way home to sleep off their exertions. There is nothing like fresh croissants and a large *café crème* to combat the effects of an early-morning hangover – as I well remember!

I turned off at the covered market in the town centre and drove round the square, parking my van in its usual place within easy reach of my regular pitch. It was the week after the Soumoulou market and the first Thursday of the month, when the Dax antiques market is held. Dax is no stranger to the English; the city experienced three centuries of English rule (1152–1453) and Richard the Lionheart is believed to have built the original castle and fortified wall, only parts of which survive. Dax is a well-known spa town and attracts large numbers of *curistes*, who come for the mud baths and natural hot water springs that run underneath it. The healing properties of the springs are reputed to have been discovered by a Roman soldier who was about to go off to war and, unable to take his rheumatic old dog with him, went to drown him in the river. The dog emerged with his rheumatism gone and acting like a puppy again. It's too good a story to ignore, whether true or not, and a larger-than-life-sized bronze statue of the legionnaire and his dog has been erected in the town.

It was six-thirty in the morning and already a few *brocanteurs* were unloading stock from their vans and setting up their stands. My friend Louis was up and busy, staggering under the weight of a heavy box of LP records, which he was hefting onto one of his tables. He gave me a welcoming grin and came over puffing to shake my hand. I was still upset from discovering we were going to have to up sticks and move but the sight of Louis cheered me up.

'Hey, John, look at this will you.' He pulled several LPs out of the box. 'I've picked up a load of Lester Young stuff when he was with Count Basie and some great Billie Holiday albums.'

He knew this would get my attention, and that I loved Billie Holiday. I couldn't resist stopping to study the sleeves and we enthused about how great she was.

'We can listen to this lot later and dig Prez and Lady Day all afternoon,' he said, slapping me enthusiastically on the back.

The pitch next to mine was already crammed with expensive-looking antiques. Glittering objets d'art were positioned on polished fruitwood desks and walnut tables. Bronze figurines of scantily clad females glowed seductively, backlit by artfully placed spotlights. A closer look at the stock would reveal that most of these were reproductions with a handful of genuine antiques mixed in to add authenticity. This stand belonged to a seriously overweight individual with a turned-up nose and small piggy eyes whom Helen and I referred to jokingly as 'Monsieur Repro', but his real name was Laurent. He always carried a big stock of reproductions which he tried to pass off as genuine antiques. The trouble was that after a while it was difficult to tell which were reproductions and which were the real antiques; everything looked fake. He gave me a wave and carried on setting up his stand.

There was some sort of commotion going on in the middle of the market. A large number of excited *brocanteurs* were crowding round, pushing and shoving, and there were cries of delight mixed with shouts of protest. Someone seemed to be selling off gear from a house clearance and torches were flashing as dealers examined the goods. I tried to ignore it all, telling myself I had no intention of stooping to such a level and getting caught in a bargain-buying frenzy, but the more shouting and whoops of delight I heard from ecstatic dealers, the more my iron resolve softened. In the end I could resist it no longer and found myself running across to join in. A young dealer I recognised from Bordeaux emerged from the scrimmage grasping an antique Venetian glass bowl and a bronze clock.

'*Fantastique!*' he exclaimed, carrying them off.

Others pushed in to take his place. I tried to squeeze in and work my way through to the front, but the mass of excited dealers was virtually impenetrable. After a bit of jostling I got a glimpse of the *brocanteur* running the sale. He was wearing a hoodie, which was pulled up over his head, hiding his face. What was I doing? Dealers were shoving each other aside using elbows and behaving like vultures or jackals all bent over their prey. I pushed my way back out of the scrum. I didn't want any bargains like this. It wasn't worth it.

It was growing lighter and as the crowd of dealers milled about there was a shout of 'Mind yer backs!' and my English friend Reg came pushing through carrying a heavy pair of decorative *chenets* (firedogs). I shouted out a greeting in English and as I did there was a cry from the middle of the crowd and a figure rose up from within the melee holding a cardboard box aloft like Aphrodite rising from the sea. The man turned and, looking across at me over the heads of the crowd, cried out, 'Oi, Johnny!'

I couldn't believe my ears! I'd have known that voice anywhere. It was Serge!

'*Qu'est-ce que tu fiches?*' (What the hell are you doing?) I shouted out.

He dropped down and disappeared and a few seconds later came pushing his way through. He ran up to me and hugged me.

'*Eh Johnny, longtemps je ne t'ai pas vu!*' (Long time since I've seen you.)

He was wringing my hand and slapping me on the back.

'Where've you been, Serge?' I asked, delighted to see him. 'I thought you were dead!'

'No, I'm not dead, Johnny. I got fed up and decided to come back home. Being retired didn't really suit me. I didn't know what to do with myself. Lying about on the beach all day – it's not all it's cracked up to be.'

I was surprised to hear this from him. His face was drawn, his hair was greyer and he looked like he'd aged.

'It's great to see you, Serge,' I said. 'Are you back for good or what?'

'Well, Johnny, it's a long story. I'll tell you all about it later, eh? I'll fill you in on the past few years. You wouldn't believe the things that have happened to me.'

We turned to look at what was left of the bargain-frenzied crowd.

The 'hoodie' was now running an impromptu auction of the remnants. A couple of women dealers were arguing vociferously about who had won the bidding on a battered doll.

'I missed all this,' said Serge, gesturing at the throng of *brocanteurs*.

The auction was degenerating into a free-for-all. The arguing women were grabbing at each other, and we watched in horror as they began pulling each other's hair. The 'hoodie' was laughing out loud, egging them on, while the men with the women were shouting at him to stop, trying to pull them apart. Someone shouted that they were calling the gendarmes.

I looked at Serge. He had gone white. The 'hoodie' was facing up to the men, trying to goad them into a fight. He pushed back his hood, the better to stand up against them, and I realised where I had seen him before. It was the flashy young dealer from Soumoulou with the light-fingered child.

'There's something important I've got to tell you, Johnny,' said Serge. He looked at me, deadly serious. 'That lad there – he's my son.'

I looked at him in amazement. 'Really? You don't say?' I felt I was about to burst into hysterical laughter.

'Can you help me get him out of here before *les flics* arrive?'

I hesitated, trying to get a grip on all this new info. I didn't really want to get involved in another of Serge's farcical ventures.

'Come on,' said Serge, pleading. 'Once he gets going like this he doesn't know when to stop.'

Reluctantly I followed him, barging our way through to the young idiot who seemed ready to take on the world. We got either side of him and dragged him away. He carried on shouting aggressively.

Once we were safely inside a bar the lad began to calm down. Serge put his arm round his shoulder. 'This is my son Didier, Johnny.' There was a touch of pride in his voice.

He nodded and we shook hands. He regarded me like he'd never seen me before.

'It's Diddy, for future reference – like P. Diddy,' he said.

I smiled and tried not to snigger. Diddy Bastarde! Ken Dodd would just love that! I couldn't wait to tell Helen.

Diddy wandered off, pulling out a wad of euros and counting them, completely unfazed. Serge was watching him with an indulgent look of fatherly pride on his face. 'He just turned up and said he was my son. Been looking for me for ages, apparently. He says he just wanted to be with his old dad. I haven't seen his mother for years. I didn't even know she was pregnant. She swears he's mine.' He paused for a moment. 'But you know, I've been thinking about getting one of those paternity tests you hear about.'

I tried hard to look sympathetic. Then he continued, more upbeat.

'He's been helping me out and I'm teaching him the trade. You know – all the wrinkles I taught you once, Johnny.'

I smiled, remembering the tricks he got up to when we were out together.

'Tell me, Johnny, what do you think? Does he look like me?'

I looked over at Diddy. He was totally absorbed, still counting his euros.

'Oh yes, Serge,' I said. 'I think he's your son all right.'

The town was coming to life. I arranged to meet up with Serge later as I had to get back and set up my stand before the first wave of *curistes* hit the market.

As I unloaded my van and arranged the stock on my tables I couldn't help marvelling at Serge's sudden return. It was so unexpected and he hadn't told me the whole story of what had happened yet. It was no good. I couldn't put it off any longer. I rang Helen.

'Guess what?' I said when she answered.

'Serge is back,' she replied.

'What? How did you know?' I was flabbergasted.

'Well, he was bound to come back some time, remember – we predicted as much,' she said.

'Yes, but how the hell did you know what I was going to say?'

'I don't know, it just came to me out of the blue.'

'Well, that's amazing,' I said. 'I never imagined he'd be here doing Dax market today. It was a total shock.'

'What about Angelique? Is she with him?'

'I'm not sure. I was too embarrassed to ask him.'

'What?! I can't believe you didn't find out. Right, if you see him later invite him over for dinner. I must find out about her – I want to know exactly what happened to them in Martinique.'

'OK, I will,' I said. 'One other thing...'

'What?'

'He's got a grown-up son in tow working with him.'

'No!' There was a moment's silence as this sunk in.

'And guess what?'

'What?'

'His name's Diddy.'

There was a snort of stifled laughter at the other end of the phone. 'You mean his name's Diddy Bastarde?' Followed by a fit of the giggles.

5

A BROKEN MAN

At Helen's insistence I had brought Serge home with me and everything had been fine until halfway through the meal, when Helen raised the subject of Angelique.

'I've been worried ever since I stopped hearing from her,' she told him. 'Is she all right?'

Serge seemed pleased to see us both, and up until then everything was normal, but this question changed all that.

'She's gone,' he said, pushing his plate away and leaning forward on the table, head in his hands. Helen reached across and when she put her arm round his shoulders all the buried emotions rushed to the surface and he began to sob uncontrollably.

Helen held him as he shook in little spasms. I could feel myself welling up, too. She gave me a wide-eyed look. What could we do? How could we make it better? When I'd invited him over for dinner, I really hadn't expected him to be in such a state. It was a bit of a shock. But Helen was handling it all much better than I was.

'What do you mean gone?' I blurted out.

'She's left me,' he said softly.

To give him his due, he was making a huge effort to control himself, wiping his eyes with the back of his sleeve and taking a swig of the Spanish brandy I had cracked open for the occasion.

'I always knew this would happen,' he spluttered. 'Let's face it; Angelique was beautiful, way too good for me, completely out of my league.' He looked up and caught my eye. 'You see, everyone knew it. What was I thinking? I must have been mad.'

'It's OK, Serge,' said Helen, 'it's not your fault.'

'No, it was my fault – don't you see it was my fault? All my fault.'

'Don't worry,' said Helen, 'you can always talk to us about it all, we're your friends.'

'Yes, I've got to tell someone.' He pulled out a voluminous red spotted handkerchief and blew his nose. 'It's my little Adrien, I don't know how much longer I can bear being parted from him.' The thought of his little son set him off again. He slumped forward and fresh silent tears ran through his fingers and plopped onto the table.

I poured another slug of Spanish brandy and pushed the glass towards him. He lifted it to his mouth with a shaking hand and swigged it back.

'We've got some ice cream,' I said, trying to cheer him up. 'Would you like some?'

Helen shook her head at me and frowned.

'Well, I just thought,' I mouthed at her. 'You know...'

'It really was my fault,' said Serge. 'That island, Martinique, is incredible, you've no idea.'

'I've heard it's beautiful there,' said Helen.

'I loved it, but what interested me was I'd never seen so many rich people. It was unbelievable. And I was envious. I wanted some of it and I saw my chance to get rich, too.'

Helen gave me a look, as if she knew what was coming.

'I had a grand scheme to start a whole new business shipping antiques over from France and selling them at extortionate prices. It couldn't fail.'

He was excited now as he relived the moment.

'And my beautiful Angelique was my *pièce de résistance*. After she had our baby, our little Adrien, we put my plan into action. You know, she still had her beautiful slim figure even after the birth and she was blooming, even more stunning than before. I got her to schmooze all the potential clients. Men swarmed round her like flies and she gave them the works. It was designer this and designer that – they had so much money. I encouraged her to chat them up because they were dripping cash and I knew I could offload tons of expensive stuff on them to put in their mansions and on their shiny yachts.'

He took another slurp of brandy and blew his nose noisily in his hankie. He sat staring into space for a moment, remembering.

'There was one guy in particular.' His voice took on a hard edge. 'He had a massive yacht like a floating palace – even had a helipad on the deck. It was amazing. He had private bodyguards and a personal trainer. He would have had Nubian slaves fanning him with palm fronds if it had been acceptable.' He gave a mocking laugh at his own joke.

'He just lured her away; I didn't stand a chance. She fell for his charms hook, line and sinker. He was rich and handsome and I sensed something was going on between them but I was greedy and ignored it. Then one day he took Adrien and Angelique out on his yacht and they never came back. I waited and waited and in the end I went to the police and they were totally unsympathetic. They just laughed. My darling Angelique had found someone younger who was more fun and who had more money than I could even dream of. He stole her away and took my son, my little Adrien – everything I cared for in the world – and sailed off into the sunset.'

That explains why the emails and phone calls from Angelique suddenly stopped, I thought.

'And who could blame her?' Serge went on. 'Look at me – what have I got to offer a woman like that?'

We both sat impotently trying to think. He was right. Put like that, it was hard to come up with anything convincing.

'Well, what about your Diddy?' I blurted out. 'He's your son as well, your long-lost son.'

He stared blankly into the middle distance. 'It's not the same, Johnny,' he said flatly. 'He's from a previous life, and frankly, I can't seem to believe he's mine.'

'You've not heard anything from Angelique since?' asked Helen. 'I mean, she can't have just disappeared.'

'I've tried to find out where they went but there's just a big wall of silence. I was desperate; I phoned everyone and just sat and waited on the marina for days on end, scanning the horizon. That handsome Lothario had completely covered his tracks. In the end I just had to give up and come back home.'

'What's he like, your Diddy?' asked Helen, trying to change the subject.

'If you've got money like that, you can do whatever you please,' said Serge, ignoring the question.

'Us miserable sods with no money or influence can go hang ourselves. We don't stand a chance. The big boys up there have got it all sewn up. They can do whatever they please, make us jump like a box full of puppets.'

'But it must have been a nice surprise for you,' Helen persisted, 'when you came back and found out about Diddy?'

It worked. Serge turned to her. 'It was amazing – he'd been searching for me all the time I was away. But you're right, it was a surprise, a big surprise. I used to live with his mother in a little village in the north of France when I was fresh out of the army. What with one thing and another it didn't work out and we split up after a couple of years. We weren't married. I was young and foolish. Her parents put a lot of pressure on us to marry. I didn't want to be tied down. I ran away down south. I didn't know she was pregnant. She brought Diddy up telling him his father was a handsome soldier and when he was older he could come and find me. And that's exactly what he's done.'

'Life has a strange way of turning things round and balancing things up, doesn't it?' I said, surprising myself by unexpectedly waxing philosophical. It was an emotional situation and I was out of my depth, unsure how to handle it. Helen was better equipped than I was. She always knew what to say. I could have done with a swig of brandy myself. It would have taken the edge off things and allowed me to relax, tackling such an emotive subject. Pity I was on the wagon.

'What about Robespierre?' I asked. And as soon as I had asked I wished I hadn't.

Serge's shoulders began to shake and he collapsed in a fit of sobbing again, blubbing like a baby.

Helen put her arms round him again and looked at me. I pulled a face and wished I'd kept my big mouth shut. But what had happened to Robespierre? I really wanted to know. He'd been a great little dog. He was given to Serge as a puppy by an old couple who were touched when we returned the body of their dog Hercules after we witnessed him being run down and killed by a hit-and-run driver. Robespierre was one of a litter of Hercules' puppies and Serge was moved to tears because Hercules was exactly like his beloved dog Danton, that had recently died. The old couple were so touched they insisted Serge take one of the puppies. Serge named him Robespierre after Maximilien

Robespierre, the bloodthirsty instigator of the Reign of Terror during the French Revolution.

Eventually Serge raised his head and looked up. His face was haunted but he was making a huge effort to pull himself together. Helen fetched a box of tissues, pulled one out, handed it to him and he blew his nose noisily.

'It's all right, Serge,' she said. 'You don't have to tell us if you don't want to.'

'No, you need to know,' he said. 'You're my friends, the only ones who'll really understand.' He made a little choking sound. 'They took him as well... they took my Robespierre with them.'

6

BERETS AND LOST SOULS

We were really upset for Serge. It was awful to see him brought so low. But although I felt sorry for him I was also pleased to have him back. I had missed him, and now I was looking forward to meeting up at the old markets, hanging out and having a laugh together. There was no getting away from it; there was never a dull moment when he was around. It would take my mind off other things, like the house move we were going to have to make.

Helen had reservations about the pair of us getting together again. 'Just think before you go along with any of his harebrained schemes this time,' she said.

'I'm not a novice *brocanteur* any more,' I assured her. 'Trust me – I know what I'm doing. I won't let him lead me astray again.'

'I'll believe that when I see it,' she said.

Helen was throwing herself into house-hunting with a vengeance. She was going out looking at houses on her own, while I always found something important to do so I was never available, hoping it might stop the whole process and we could stay put. She got in touch with banks and brokers who might give us a *prêt relais* (bridging loan) so we could buy a house if we found one we liked and have time to sell ours. She put our house up for sale with every estate agent she could. Everyone who came to view our house was enchanted by it, but as soon as they heard a *lotissement* was going to be built on the adjoining field they never came back for a second look. I was secretly pleased and worried sick at the same time. So when I saw Serge at Anglet market, just outside Bayonne, and he told me he had been tipped off about a special private auction of the contents of a *maison de retraite* (retirement home) outside Lourdes I thought it would be the perfect distraction for us both and give me and Helen a break from all the stress.

'You should both come along,' said Serge. 'It's not been advertised and none of the big Bordeaux or Toulouse dealers will be there. Could be a good one.'

Lourdes! I was already thinking about visiting the museum of berets which is in the little village of Nay, not far from the town. If we went to the sale, I could nip in. I had wanted to visit since passing it on our first trip to Lourdes. Why should we English find a museum of berets so amusing? My French friends don't find it at all funny. I mentioned it to Serge but he was unfazed. 'Ah yes, Johnny, the Musée du Béret, very interesting.'

'Very interesting? What could be interesting about a museum of berets to you? I've never seen you wearing one,' I said.

'No, but it's a symbol of *La France*. We may not all wear one but every Frenchman loves the beret. It's like you English and your *chapeau melon*.'

'We don't all love bowler hats,' I said. 'In fact, to people of my age – the post-war baby boomers who became the sixties generation – the bowler hat is a boring symbol of conformity and lack of imagination. You seldom see a bowler hat in England any more.'

Serge looked confused. He couldn't really grasp this.

'Well, it's just a few local dealers and us who'll be there, so keep it under your beret,' he said, chuckling at his own joke.

To the French the bowler hat represents all things British and they find it very funny for some reason. He couldn't comprehend that we might view the beret in a similar way. Also, the French have little museums all over the place. Apart from the Musée du Béret there is also the Musée du Pruneau (the plum museum) in the Lot. That's another unmissable day out. Forget Alton Towers or Disneyland, take the kids to the plum museum – they'll love it!

Helen's friend Karen bought a holiday home in the Lot and was taken out for a special treat by her *agricole* neighbours to a melon festival. She said it was the longest and most boring day she had ever spent in her life and she kept thinking to herself: 'I'll never get this time back – ever.' But her neighbours were engrossed. She couldn't believe the thrill they got from expounding the virtues of the many different types of melon. Tomato festivals are also a popular attraction all over France every year. And yes, there are even quite a few tomato museums.

Could it be that the English in their urbanised society are simply overstimulated? We use the word 'boring' to describe so many simple pursuits from which the French derive great pleasure. Mention *champignons* (mushrooms) to anyone French and watch their eyes light up. They love nothing better than to discuss the various merits of *cèpes*, *bolets*, *girolles*, how and where to find them, and the best recipes for cooking and serving them. There are several large societies for mushroom identification and gathering. Foraging for mushrooms is a national pastime. They are surprised when we show no interest in joining them.

And what are the things in combination that typically identify a Frenchman to the rest of the world? A beret, a bottle of wine, a baguette? In the eyes of the American jazzmen of the forties and the beat generation of the sixties the beret was considered both hip and cool. Two of my heroes, bebop jazzman Dizzy Gillespie and pianist Thelonious Monk, sported berets, as did Pablo Picasso, Che Guevara and all of the Black Panther movement. In the punk era Captain Sensible of The Damned was seldom seen without his bright red beret. My Uncle Den, who was a veteran of the parachute regiment and was dropped behind enemy lines in France during World War Two, always wore his red beret too, right up until he died in his eighties. The Nazis couldn't kill him but a superbug did when he was briefly hospitalised after falling over at home.

I had toyed with the idea of wearing a beret myself when I found one in an old armoire I was restoring. I thought I looked quite good in it. Wearing it at a jaunty angle I imagined myself as a hipster from Jack Kerouac's *On the Road*. But Helen, when she'd stopped laughing, said I looked 'a right twat' and gave me an affectionate kiss. So that was that, then. A beret wasn't for me. But when Serge, Helen and I arrived for the sale the following week I decided to visit the Musée du Béret anyway.

I left Helen at the sale while I nipped across to Nay to visit the museum.

'I can't think of anything more boring than a beret museum,' had been Helen's comment. In the event she was right; it wasn't as heart-stoppingly exciting as I had expected. But it was interesting to learn about the history of berets and all the different types. One model that has always fascinated me is the huge floppy sort much favoured by Basques. It can sometimes look like a bit of a joke. I'd even seen young French people burst into fits of uncontrollable laughter on being confronted with some old boy wearing one. I hadn't realised that these caricature berets were *le béret chasseur* (hunter's beret) or possibly *le béret extra large* (extra big beret) – ideal for keeping the head dry in a rainstorm when you're hunting, or in the case of *le béret extra large*, if you've got a big head.

I drove back to Lourdes. The last time I'd been here was when we visited St Bernadette's grotto and Robespierre, Serge's dog, was amazingly healed by the holy water.

The *maison de retraite* was a whitewashed building set in beautiful rambling grounds on the outskirts of the town. There appears to be a strangely sanctified atmosphere enveloping the town of Lourdes. I am not fond of organised religion but here there is a feeling of calm and tranquillity. As I wandered among the trees and flowering shrubs I could hear the auction going on in the house through an open window. Outside in the garden it was calm and peaceful. *What an ideal setting for a retirement home,* I thought, *and what a shame it is closing down.*

I was admiring a particularly beautiful magnolia tree, magnificent in full bloom, when in the distance I saw Lord Snooty striding across the garden towards me. Oh no! He'd seen me and it was too late to hide. I tried to remember Snooty's real name. I had noticed of late that my memory wasn't what it was. I'd put it down to an excessive intake of alcohol in my youth which had destroyed the brain cells. This always puts me in mind of the Lewis Carroll parody verse, 'You Are Old Father William', from *Alice In Wonderland*:

'"In my youth," Father William replied to his son,

"I feared it might injure the brain;

But now I am perfectly sure I have none,

Why, I do it again and again."'

The last time I'd seen Snooty was at Soumoulou when he'd upset Thibaut with his racist remarks about the French. It suddenly came back to me... Algie! That was his name.

He came over and greeted me like a long-lost pal. I got the impression he had decided I was a proper public-school-educated Englishman and a natural ally.

'Great to see you, old chap,' he enthused. 'How are you?'

'Good, thanks, Algie,' I said. 'How's it going with you, Algie, all right?' I enjoyed saying the name. The only Algies I'd heard of were in Rupert the Bear or P. G. Wodehouse books.

'Don't blame you staying out here,' he said. 'Crap is going for silly money. I'm going to bugger off soon, there's nothing of any real quality here for me.'

'Helen, my wife, is in there buying,' I explained. 'I'm just waiting for the sale to finish to pick up what she's bought.'

'She's that attractive redhead, isn't she? Reg told me she was your wife. She's outbid me on a couple of pieces I wanted. Maybe we Brits can come to some arrangement between the three of us.'

'Maybe,' I said. But I was thinking 'not likely'. There was no way we were going to try to ring sales, and especially not with him.

As I approached the building I saw a familiar figure in tracksuit and trainers leaning against the front door smoking a roll-up. It was Gerard, a *gitan* (gypsy) friend I hadn't seen for ages. He and his wife Josette drove around in a removals van with a huge Basque flag painted on the side and had a mobile home parked on a few hectares of land in the nearby foothills of the Pyrenees where they kept goats, chickens and a couple of ponies. But I'd heard they had hit hard times.

'Eh, Johnny.' He seized my hand and wrung it, smiling through his craggy broken teeth.

'How are you?' I asked.

'You know, things aren't so good, Johnny. You heard we had to sell our place?'

'I didn't know that,' I said.

'Yes, it broke our hearts. It was really tough. We had to get rid of our ponies – that was the hardest part. I've bought a second-hand caravan and we're back to travelling around between *gitan* sites, working the markets.'

I sympathised with him. I knew how much his land had meant to him.

'How has Josette taken it?' I asked.

'Not good, Johnny. She's inside, bidding. She'd like to see you, I'm sure.'

'I'll go and say hello,' I said.

'She's bidding for dolls.' He shrugged, like he couldn't see the attraction.

'There are some nice ones, are there?' I asked.

'Dolls?' he said, shrugging again. 'Our mobile home was full of them and now you can't move in the caravan for dolls as it's even smaller. Our kids are grown up with families of their own, but Josette's always after more dolls. When we were up against it I begged her to sell off some of them as they're worth money, but she wouldn't hear of it – they're like babies to her. There's barely any space left for me to sit down without squashing one.'

I sympathised with him. I'm not a great doll lover myself – I find them a bit creepy – but I was aware of the power they exerted over some people, especially obsessive doll collectors. Helen had begun buying them in auctions and they seemed to sell well. Also, I was remembering a little wooden devil Gerard had once given me, and how unsettling that had been.

'Coming in?' he asked, pinching out his roll-up. He pulled out an old tobacco tin and stowed the stub away for future use. He was a proud man and I felt my heart go out to him. He and Josette had chosen to settle down – never an easy decision for people from a *gitan* background – and through no fault of their own it hadn't worked out. Now they were having to readjust and be drawn back to their old way of life. I hoped it worked out for them. We went in together and stood at the back of a small throng of dealers and private buyers in the hall. I felt an elbow in my ribs and turned to see Reg's grinning face.

'Blimey, you and your missus get about. You're a long way from your stomping grounds, aren't you?'

'Serge tipped me off about this one,' I said. 'He assured me there wouldn't be many dealers here.'

'He gives you some good tips doesn't he, old Sergey? Yeah, well the Bordeaux and Toulouse mob are all here, they never miss out. I saw old Snooty earlier. I wouldn't have thought it was his scene. I'll tell you what, though – if he wants a load of old antique bedpans, he's come to the right place.' He snorted with laughter.

'You haven't seen Serge, have you?' I asked.

'He was around earlier, but Diddy, that son of his, is up front bidding like there's no tomorrow. Hope it's not Serge's dosh he's spending, 'cos he hasn't a clue what he's doing.'

'Diddy's here bidding without Serge?' I was surprised.

Helen was pushing her way back through the crowd. She gave me a wave, excusing herself to the other dealers as she shoved past. She grabbed me and gave me a hug.

'Have we got any money left?' I said.

'It's not been cheap but I've got some good stuff – you wait till you see it. They're going to auction off the dining room furniture next. There's a massive oak table in there that we couldn't move with the help of ten men, let alone store it anywhere – it must weigh a ton.'

'Don't buy that then,' I said. 'I haven't got a hernia yet, touch wood, but my back's not what it used to be.'

'Don't worry, I won't,' she reassured me, smiling.

I was tempted to remind her of the huge corn hopper she bought on a whim in a farm sale in England when we first started out in antiques. It weighed a ton and there was no way I could shift the damn thing. In the end I had to leave it there in the middle of the field. But the last time I'd mentioned it she got very annoyed, so I thought it best not to bring it up again. It was a bit of a cheap shot.

We tagged along behind as the crowd moved into the dining room and then, once the furniture was sold off, followed everyone downstairs into the basement for the wine and kitchenalia. As we squeezed down the narrow stairwell I spotted Reg and Algie squashed together, following the flow. Reg made a remark I couldn't quite catch and Algie gave a horsey laugh. He hadn't 'buggered off' then.

The shift to downstairs had livened everyone up and there was a buzz of conversation as the young, fresh-faced auctioneer restarted the proceedings. He was acting like a head prefect at school, shouting out orders in the face of total anarchy. The auction had degenerated into an excuse for everyone to have a light hearted chat and enjoy themselves, and the more he tried to reassert his authority the less it was heeded.

Gerard was just ahead of us with Josette, who was clutching an antique doll under one arm. She saw me and came over to give me and Helen kisses on both cheeks. She was evidently enjoying herself and I got a whiff of heady perfume as she turned back and carried on gossiping with an old *gitan* woman with a blue rinse and gold earrings. Gerard squeezed between me and Helen. 'That's Josette's mother,' he confided. 'She's over eighty. She's a live one, she is; she insists on coming everywhere with us and loves sales.'

The auctioneer was getting hoarse, shouting for calm. His face was red and he was losing it. 'Quiet!' he yelled above the hubbub. 'I can't carry on with all this noise! Shut up!'

71

There was a brief lull in the conversation, and then the commotion started up again, even louder than before.

This time his temper exploded. 'If you don't shut up, next time any of you have guests I'll come over to your houses and dance on the table shouting!'

There was total silence for a moment, suddenly broken by a small, frail voice.

'And will you be wearing a thong?' It was Josette's mother.

There was a roar of laughter, complete pandemonium. Any possibility of the auctioneer regaining control had gone. Dealers reached over to pat Josette's mother on the back. The women were hysterical, shouting at the auctioneer and describing to each other how they imagined he would look in a thong.

Helen was laughing, too. She squeezed my hand. 'We can go upstairs now and pick up some of the stuff we've bought. It's OK, there's nothing down here we want anyway.'

We worked our way through the raucous crowd, up the back stairs and onwards up a wide, winding staircase to the first floor. This *maison de retraite* was magnificent. There were long halls with high windows at each end overlooking the gardens. Running off the passages were tastefully decorated bedrooms and small dormitories. I couldn't understand how such a pleasant old people's home could be closed down like this. It seemed almost sacrilegious.

Helen led me through to a small dormitory. 'I've bought this bed in here.' She pointed to a bed with *chevets* (pot cupboards – sometimes referred to as 'bedside tables' by antique dealers).

'I'll dismantle the bed then, shall I?' I said. As luck would have it I'd brought my special little tool with me for unscrewing the bolts on these ancient beds, and I set to it on my hands and knees.

'I'm going downstairs,' said Helen. 'You'll be all right here?'

'I'll be fine,' I assured her, grunting as I tried to shift a stiff bolt. I managed to disassemble the bed and started off along the corridor carrying the large wooden headboard, intending to load it into our van.

As I made my way along the dimly lit passageway past the open bedroom doors I suddenly had a strange vision. I felt there were confused old people leaning out from those doorways looking at me, wondering what I was doing. In my mind's eye they appeared deeply disturbed, as if they weren't sure what was going on. It was a strange feeling, strong and quite vivid. It reminded me of the time after my Uncle Tom had died and I went with Helen to see my Auntie Elsie. I had an overpowering feeling he was there in the room welcoming me and overjoyed to see me. I sat in his chair and could sense him standing beside me, beaming as my auntie chatted away. Was I dreaming up these lost souls? It didn't feel like it. They seemed very real and I found myself talking softly in French to them as I passed, assuring them that everything was fine and they shouldn't worry. I remembered how I had done the same thing, reassuring

Gaston, the deceased previous owner of our house, that we meant no harm in our farmhouse when I had knocked down the interior wall. I must be losing my grip on reality.

I met Helen on the stairs on her way up to see me and told her about it.

'Do you think I'm going mad?'

'Yes,' she replied, matter-of-factly.

'Actually, I had a similar feeling earlier,' said Helen. 'I was on my own and went into a room to see what was in there. I had the feeling I wasn't alone, that someone had come in. I turned to say *"bonjour"* and there was no one there.'

I told her I didn't find it frightening, but that I felt sad that they were so lost and worried.

When I returned for the rest of the bed I thought the feeling might have evaporated but it was just as strong.

As I loaded the bed and *chevets* into the van I saw Serge coming towards me. He too looked bewildered. But as he got nearer I realised he was not so much confused as annoyed. He was cursing like an expert, spitting out expletives.

'Do you know what that son of mine has done now, Johnny?'

I said I didn't, as I had been upstairs dismantling a bed.

'Did you see that massive oak table in the dining room?'

'Helen told me about it, it's a big one, isn't it?'

'Big? It's giant-sized,' he moaned. 'It'll take about eight men to shift and it will never go in my van. Diddy paid well over the odds for it and he expects me to cough up and foot the bill. I tried to tell the auctioneer I don't want it but he says Diddy bought it fair and square and he won't re-auction it now.'

'What are you going to do?'

'And that's not all, Johnny,' he continued, ignoring my question, 'he's bought a load more stuff. Bedpans! Who wants bedpans these days?'

'Sick people?' I offered.

'Yes, but I've got two hundred of them. Do you need one yourself, maybe? I can let you have a couple dead cheap.' He made a noise halfway between a laugh and a groan.

'I don't know, he doesn't seem to have a clue that boy. He's going to ruin me. He's not got the sense he was born with.'

'Oh, come on,' I said. 'He's not that bad, surely; you told me last week it was nice having your son working alongside you.'

'I thought it would be, yes. But sometimes I can't believe a son of mine would be so clueless. He doesn't take after me, that's for sure.'

'No, perhaps not, but he's inherited your spirit of enterprise, Serge,' I said, trying to cheer him up.

'Do you think so?' He was flattered. 'Well, OK, maybe I can shift those bedpans as trendy flower pots, or perhaps wine coolers.' He was perking up visibly at the thought.

'Mmmm.' I nodded and smiled. 'You could be on to something there, Serge.'

... Not! Rustics who still kept potties under the bed for relieving themselves in the night tended to snigger uncontrollably at the sight of a potty being offered for sale as a desirable antique. How would they react to bedpans?

'I meant to ask you, Johnny, how was the Musée du Béret? I bet you enjoyed yourself while poor Helen was working away here on her own trying to grab a bargain.'

'It was quite interesting,' I conceded. 'But not as much as a Musée du Chapeau Melon would have been to us English.'

Serge found this remark incredibly funny. He exploded with hysterical laughter. When he eventually managed to regain control he took one look at me and he was off again, slapping his knees, pointing at my deadpan expression.

'You English are so funny! What a sense of humour, eh?' He wiped his eyes.

'I'd love to see you in a *chapeau melon*, Johnny. If I ever see one on the markets, I'm going to buy it for you.'

'Don't bother,' I said. 'The only way I'd ever don a *chapeau melon* is if I was wearing a codpiece with one eye made-up like Alex in *A Clockwork Orange*.'

He looked at me, baffled. I'd lost him on that one.

'Hang on a moment though, Johnny, I have got something to show you that I'm sure you'll appreciate.' He jumped into the back of his van and I heard him banging about before he emerged with what looked like an old brown fibre box. He undid the strap and pulled something out wrapped in tissue paper. It was round and made of a blue woollen material and looked suspiciously like a beret!

'This came up in the sale with some other hats today and I couldn't resist buying it.'

He removed the tissue paper and carefully positioned the beret on his head.

'Well, what do you think?' He struck what he intended to be a noble pose. 'It suits me, doesn't it?'

I looked at him in amazement. It suited him, all right. The beret was huge and floppy and stuck out prominently like the top of a giant drooping blue mushroom. He was proudly sporting a classic version of *le béret extra large*, the one that was ideal for people with big heads.

'I like it!' I said, trying to keep a straight face.

7

WOODWORM AND WALNUT BUFFETS

We sat and stared balefully at the beautiful walnut buffet that Diddy had originally sold to a rich customer, who had returned it, complaining it was 'making strange noises in the night'. Serge said he thought it was some sort of wood-boring beetle at work and we had to annihilate it. We had taken the doors off and lain the top half with its little carved wooden figures and ornate finials against the wall in Serge's garage. It was around midnight and we strained our ears to hear, hardly daring to breathe.

And there it was – a kind of crunch, crunch, crunching sound. It was hard to tell where the noise was coming from exactly. But it appeared to be from somewhere deep inside the wood.

Serge got down on his hands and knees and put his ear up close. He cupped one hand and listened, moving his head up and down, trying to pinpoint it. After several minutes of this he shook his head and stood up.

'That young idiot! I've told him so many times. If there are holes, treat it. Kill the little beggars, because if you don't,' he waved at the buffet, 'you're going to be left with sawdust.' He sat down on a chaise longue with horsehair sprouting through holes in its velour cover and put his head in his hands.

Since he had told us about his break-up with Angelique, his separation from his baby boy Adrien and his dog Robespierre, I had begun to see Serge as vulnerable. I felt sorry for him and tried to help him whenever I could.

'Can't you just give the man his money back?' I asked.

He lifted his head and gave me a look that suggested I was born yesterday.

'Give it back? Give the money back? No, of course he can't give it back! The little idiot's spent it. You think Diddy has any money to give back to people? He's up the casino gambling it away or on the Internet buying clothes. He can never give any money back. It burns a hole in his pocket. He's got no idea of the value of it. Besides, the guy who bought this is a real heavy with contacts all over Eastern Europe. You see all these other pieces?' He pointed to several *chevets*, chandeliers and wrought-iron lamps. 'He's filling a container of French antiques and exporting it to his warehouse out there. I've got to pack a load of my better stuff in boxes for transportation. He wants the stuff cheap but he can shift a lot of antiques so it's worth it to me.'

We had picked up the buffet earlier that evening in Biarritz from the man who had complained about the noises it was making.

'This guy is rich,' Serge confided, 'and when I say rich I mean *rupin*, filthy rich.' He rubbed his thumb and forefinger together. 'And he's powerful, too. I can't afford to offend him. He'd have me done – just like that.' He smacked his hands together as if he were killing a bug.

'It was Bruno who put me onto him. He's a really good contact. I've got to keep him sweet.'

This information about the link with Bruno made me feel uneasy. I had come up against Serge's dubious friend Bruno the Basque in the past and I had an intense dislike of the man.

Serge's rich client owned a smart penthouse apartment in Biarritz. We had gone up in the lift and rung his doorbell on the eighth floor. We stood outside the door waiting in the plush hallway.

'This is impressive,' I said to Serge.

'Yeah, well he's a Romanian, he likes things just so.'

'A Romanian? You didn't tell me he was Romanian. Does he speak French?'

The door swung open to reveal a man dressed in a turquoise towelling dressing gown and blue silk pyjamas. It was four in the afternoon. He was tanned with silver-grey hair combed back like a fifties thug. He looked like the sort of grumpy, tough person you wouldn't want to annoy. He signalled impatiently for us to enter and we followed him through into a sumptuously decorated living room with a panoramic view over the sea. We both stood, spellbound, watching the boats go by.

'Right, you two clowns,' said the grumpy old man, breaking our reverie. He spoke with a strong Eastern European accent 'That whoring thing, it keeps on going tap-tap-tap night and day. It is driving me crazy. Get it fixed. I don't care how you do it, just do it!'

'Don't worry, sir,' said Serge obsequiously, 'my colleague here and I will sort it out. We'll take it back to my workshop and find out what the trouble is.'

The man was unimpressed. 'You better.' He glowered.

Serge grovelled pathetically and promised it would all be fine, and we hefted the buffet through the dining room, trying not to bump into any of the incredibly valuable pieces of antique furniture that adorned the flat. On the way to the front door we hit the wall and ripped a piece out of the expensive designer wallpaper. Serge hurriedly licked his finger and stuck back the telltale tear. We tried to manoeuvre the buffet through the front door and in doing so scratched the paintwork and scuffed the polished wood of the buffet.

The front door was slammed after us and when the lift arrived I realised we had no chance of getting the buffet in it, but Serge insisted we turn it this way and that, trying to squeeze it through the sliding doors. It didn't help that every time we pulled it out, ready to try again, the lift door slid shut and descended to pick up someone below who had pushed the button. Serge began cursing and shouting to whoever was down there to stop it.

It was hard to convince him we were going to have to hump the buffet down eight flights of stairs, but in the end he conceded we had no choice. Around the fourth floor the strain began to get to me and I found myself singing Bernard Cribbins' 'Right Said Fred'.

'What's that damn thing you keep singing?' asked Serge, puffing as we negotiated the winding stairway.

'Oh, nothing much,' I said. 'It's an English song about moving a piano, that's all.'

'Pianos! Don't talk to me about pianos! I got a hernia moving bloody pianos. Thank God no one wants those sods any more.'

We managed to get the buffet to the ground floor, load it into Serge's van and drive it to his apartment, where he had spent most of the evening in his garage squirting a smelly woodworm treatment into all the little woodworm holes.

'These holes are mostly old,' he said now. 'I can't see why there would be live worm in here.'

The treatment consisted of an aerosol can with a clear plastic tube with a needle on one end. The needle was inserted into a hole and the button on the can pressed, whooshing a thin spray of deadly killing liquid deep down along the tiny passageway to where the worm was supposedly hiding. Serge had lost the small protective funnel which fitted round the needle. When he pressed the button the deadly fluid went deep down the entrance hole and out an adjacent exit hole, spraying him unexpectedly in the face. He leapt back like he'd been stung, frantically rubbing his eyes. He ran to the bathroom and reappeared a few minutes later. His eyes were red and he kept blinking. He continued his work with the aerosol but this time leant back so when the liquid sprayed out it missed his face. I kept dodging the spurts as I held the buffet steady.

We stopped for a coffee and Serge had a Ricard with his. We examined the buffet again.

'See this one here?' Serge pointed out an impressive hole a few centimetres across. 'That's where a Capricorn came out. The grubs have got massive jaws. I think that's what could be making the noise.'

I'd seen these Capricorn beetles. They were beautiful. About the same size or slightly bigger than an English stag beetle, only more streamlined, with great long antennae that curved out and round either side. They were a species of longhorn beetle, so-called as the antennae resembled the curving horns of a mountain sheep.

I decided to go and ring Helen again. Earlier I'd phoned to tell her we'd picked up a buffet from Serge's Romanian client. She'd sounded surprised.

'Romanian? That's interesting, does he speak French then?'

'Yes, he's a nice bloke,' I lied.

'Nice? What sort of nice?' She smelt a rat.

We had noticed Eastern Europeans gradually arriving in France over the past few years and others travelling down into Spain. They had increased in number and some seemed to be lost, ill at ease and out of step with the modern world. Many had integrated quickly, learnt French and set up and ran very successful businesses, but others were outside society. Over time it was these begging Eastern Europeans that were the only ones everyone noticed, talked about and objected to, and the hardworking majority was overlooked. Helen and I had been travelling back from a sale in the van one time, our clothes all dusty from collecting items we had bought in a barn, when we were flagged down. French laws oblige you to stop and help if someone is in difficulty and this was a family in trouble on a country road. We pulled over only to be harassed for our bank card, purportedly to buy petrol, by a tough character and his thuggish son. They wanted me to take them to a cash machine. Luckily we had neither cards nor money on us and we looked so poor they lost interest when one of the family managed to stop another car. Most of the French are wise to these scams and drive past unconcerned. I had to admit I did have a nagging feeling of unease about Serge's client.

I promised Helen I wouldn't be much longer. She was keen to tell me about a house she had looked at. I went back to help Serge in his garage.

He was bent over the buffet intent on the job in hand, examining the large Capricorn hole. 'I reckon if we cut out this piece of wood here and follow the tunnel down we'll find the little swine making all the noise,' he said. 'The woodworm killer doesn't seem to affect him. He's probably so tough he's immune to it.' He fetched a vicious-looking pointed saw.

'Is that such a good idea?' I said. 'Maybe we should just wait for the treatment to work.'

'No, Johnny, trust me. He's in there, all right. It's just a question of cutting him out like a cancer. He'll never crunch again once I get to him.'

He began sawing vigorously on either side of the large hole. Eventually he gave up and fetched a mini electric drill with a box of small bits and saw wheels. He affixed a nasty-looking cutting implement, plugged in the machine, set it running and attacked the buffet anew. It made a scary searing noise, which reminded me of a dentist's drill. The expression on Serge's face was disconcerting, too. When I was a kid my mum took me and my brother to a dentist called Mr Walmsley in Kingston who had a similar expression when he was drilling your teeth. His drill wasn't much more sophisticated than the one Serge was using, and it vibrated and sent screaming shafts of agonising pain through your raw nerves. My brother, who was three years younger than me, had been unable to stand it and bit into Mr Walmsley's hand, drawing blood. We changed our dentist soon after that.

The tunnel was longer than Serge expected. Soon there was a big chunk out of the wood and a little pile of sawdust on the floor. He began poking about in the hole with a screwdriver and after a moment let out a cry of triumph. A huge bloated white grub plopped out and fell amongst the splintered pieces of wood. He dropped down on his hands and knees and scrabbled about in the sawdust until he held the thing aloft grasped between his thumb and forefinger. It twisted and turned in its nudity like a peeled prawn.

'There you are, my little beauty.' He placed it on the concrete floor and before I could stop him, brought his heel down on it hard. It exploded with a loud pop, sending a squirt of disgusting glop all over his jeans. He pulled a face and tried to wipe off the mess with an old hankie, but only succeeded in spreading it into a large unsightly stain.

'The buffet's not too bad. I can graft a piece in there later, he'll never notice,' he said confidently.

He removed the drawers and the pair of walnut doors and leant them against the garage wall. We stood listening again, hardly daring to draw breath. All was quiet. The crunching sound had stopped.

'That's it then, it was that little bugger all the time,' he said, wiping at the yellow gunge on his jeans.

'Well, I'd better be off,' I said, standing up to leave. 'Helen's expecting me back.' It was way past midnight and I was anxious to get home.

'OK, Johnny, you go. Maybe you could give me a hand getting this back to my client. I'll get Diddy to help us tomorrow. It'll be easier with the three of us.'

I was halfway to the door when I stopped. What was that? It couldn't be! But there it was again – the crunching sound. Only this time it was even louder. Serge was up in a flash, saw in hand. I thought he was going to attack it willy-nilly, but he knelt over the buffet, head to one side, listening. The look of desperation on his face was unsettling.

'There must be another one in there. If we can kill one, then we can get the other. It's here, I'm sure of it,' he said, pointing at a carved leg. 'I could just cut him out. It won't take a minute.'

I thought about trying to dissuade him. But I was exhausted and he wouldn't have taken any notice. He took my tired expression as one of agreement and began to attack the leg ferociously with the electric saw. Soon it was in pieces on the floor and the buffet was leaning to one side. He turned off the saw and listened. Nothing. Silence. Then we heard it again. The steady crunch, crunch, crunching sound.

It was then that Serge lost it. He grabbed a handsaw, a hammer and chisel and began dismantling the beautiful walnut buffet plank by plank. I watched helplessly as he piled up the pieces. Every so often he stopped to listen and move the bits about. And when he established the crunching hadn't stopped he carried on sawing and chiselling.

I couldn't take any more. Bits of the beautiful walnut buffet were strewn all over the garage. 'I'm going,' I said, and began to pick my way through the debris to the door.

'Stop and have a coffee before you go, Johnny, I feel in need of a bit of support here. Diddy doesn't normally roll home until the early hours of the morning,' pleaded Serge.

How could I refuse? He looked pathetic. He went through to the kitchen while I sat on the chaise longue listening to

SON OF SERGE BASTARDE

him clattering about. He brought in the coffees and we sat drinking them, staring at the mess.

Suddenly I noticed a tiny movement in the sawdust near my foot. A piece of splintered wood began to rock almost imperceptibly. A large black beetle emerged and slowly began to make its way across the concrete floor. It was unmistakably a Capricorn, its longhorn antennae clearly visible. Serge saw it too and gripped my arm. We watched, fascinated, as it scuttled away, picking up speed as it headed off in search of pastures new. Serge gave a cry, whipped off his shoe and charged after it, taking a flying leap. But the beetle had reached the beams in the wall and with an uncanny sixth sense found a crack in the woodwork and disappeared into it. Serge brought his shoe down with a loud thwack but it was too late – the insect had escaped.

He hopped back, his shoe hanging limply at his side. I passed him his coffee and he sipped at it. 'That Capricorn will lay its eggs in there,' he said. 'The whole place will be infested.'

'What's he going to say, your rich client, when he finds out you've totally destroyed his beautiful walnut buffet?'

'I don't know, what can he say? He'll probably have me killed and my body parts cemented into a Spanish motorway flyover somewhere.' He gave a crazed laugh.

'You'll have to give him his money back.'

'I'll have to find it from somewhere, if I want to stay alive. I don't know how, though. I don't have that sort of money.

Diddy did the deal and he charged that guy a fortune, but I never saw a *cent* of it.'

We sat sipping our coffee, contemplating the fact. I half expected to hear the sound of crunching coming from behind the beams, but I imagined the beetle would be settling in first, checking out a whole new world of unexplored wood before it began to lay its eggs.

'That's that then, I really ought to be getting home,' I said, making another attempt to leave. I began to pick my way gingerly through the broken pieces of the buffet. There was a noise in the hall upstairs, a key in a lock, the sound of the front door opening and footsteps walking about in the apartment. Serge looked up and listened expectantly. Then there was the sound of someone coming down the stairs to the garage, the door swung open with a bang and Diddy walked in. He seemed pleasantly surprised to see me and came straight over and greeted me like a long-lost brother.

'Johnny, qu'est-ce qui ce passe?' (What's happening, man?) He shook me by the hand, effusive and full of bonhomie. He was well oiled.

He turned to see Serge, sitting in the chair surrounded by the debris from the walnut buffet.

'Eh, Papa!' He shimmied over, put his arms round him and gave him a hug.

'My Papa, my dear old Papa! Where you been all my life?'

Serge looked across at me, embarrassed. He stood up and patted Diddy on the back as if he wasn't sure how to react. Diddy swung round and beamed at me.

'What the pair of you doing out here in the garage, man?' He smiled fondly at his dad. 'You should be in bed, Papa, it's way past your bedtime.' This struck him as funny and he gave a little giggle. He looked down, noticed the bits of broken buffet scattered about and his eyes widened.

'You two been breaking up the happy home? Man, you're sure making a mess in here!'

Serge opened his mouth as if to say something.

Diddy picked up a piece of the shattered buffet and held it up close to his eyes, turning it slowly, examining it. He reached down, picked up another piece and inspected it. He turned to Serge, confused.

'What's this, Dad?'

'You don't recognise it?' said Serge. He was simmering gently.

'Nah, man, it's wood... pieces of wormy old wood.'

Serge gave me a look, raising his eyebrows.

'Right then,' I said. 'Helen will be wondering where I am.'

I started for the door and stopped. There was a woman standing in the doorway. She was stooping slightly and appeared unsteady on her feet. This could have been something to do with the stack heel shoes she was wearing. She entered the garage and tottered forward, grabbing my arm for support. Up close I could see she was a woman of a certain age – well past seventy, if I had to hazard a guess. Her face was caked with make-up, her lipstick was blood red and her eyes were thick with dark eyeliner. She was a dead ringer for Bette Davis in *Whatever Happened to Baby Jane?* She smiled coquettishly and her perfume was overpowering. Diddy was grinning at us like he was party to some private joke. 'That'll do, Claudette, this good man is off home to see his wife.'

She stopped, frozen for a moment, and stepped back.

'It's OK, Johnny,' said Serge. 'Claudette lives next door. She's a very conscientious worker, a real professional.'

'She's a *pute*,' said Diddy matter-of-factly (a whore). 'This man is from England,' he said. He had raised his voice. 'He's a *brocanteur*. He lives here in France.'

Claudette looked surprised. Her expressions were exaggerated, as if she were starring in a silent movie.

'He's English,' said Diddy. 'You know... England!'

Claudette treated his patronising manner with the contempt it deserved.

'I have many English friends.' She trailed off, remembering. 'I like English people. They have manners.' She shot Diddy a look. 'They know how to treat a lady.' She stood up straight.

'You are fond of France?' she asked.

'Yes, I like it here,' I said.

'I love English things,' she said quietly. 'You English have so much class.'

I nodded and smiled, acknowledging the compliment.

'I have English furniture in my home.'

'Oh, really?' I said.

'Yes, but I have too many things. I have a beautiful English writing bureau I wish to sell. Would you like to take a look at it? It is of top quality.'

'I'm actually off home,' I said. 'My wife is expecting me.'

She looked disappointed. 'Are you sure? It wouldn't take a moment to look.'

'I really ought to go,' I said. 'I am late already.'

She was deflated. She pulled a little face with pouted lips.

'I could come back later,' I said. 'In the day, maybe.'

She looked at me with wide eyes.

'It's been nice meeting you,' I said, starting for the door.

'Let him go, Claudette,' said Diddy. 'It's past his bedtime.'

She came after me, taking me by the arm. 'Yes, come back like you said... in the day. Bring your wife; I should like to meet her.'

'I will,' I said. 'I'll do that.'

She gave my arm a squeeze. 'We could have tea... and scones.'

8

LIFE IN A BOX

Helen was upset that I had returned so late. She had seen a house she liked and wanted me to visit it with her the next day. But I pointed out I would be at Dax market all day and I had promised to help Serge with his items for the Romanian's container in the evening. 'Wouldn't tomorrow be OK?' I asked. 'What's the rush?' It was another case of me shaping awkward as my heart wasn't really in the move.

Later that evening, after the market had packed up, I felt rotten and I began to regret not going with her. *How did I ever let Serge talk me into this one?* I thought as we climbed up a metal-runged ladder on the side of a giant skip round the back of a furniture and electrical warehouse. We were on a quest for jumbo-sized cardboard boxes. Since Serge had destroyed the beautiful walnut buffet he had been terrified of being found out. 'I've managed to stall that Romanian guy

SON OF SERGE BASTARDE

but he wants me to box up a load of furniture I promised him ready to pack in his container,' he said. 'If we drive out to Conforama on the *zone commerciale*, we're sure to find some old packing cases big enough for antique furniture,' he had assured me. Conforama is the name of a chain of retail warehouses with branches right across France.

But up here, straddling the edge of the metal skip, I wasn't so sure this was a good idea. 'There are some good ones in here Johnny, come on.'

Orange sodium light shone down on us and in the distance I could hear homeward-bound traffic on the *rocade* (ring road) as I clung to the icy rungs, pulling myself up step by step.

'See? There – just what I'm after.' He pointed into the far corner of the skip.

'Yes, but how do we get down there?' This was the biggest skip I'd ever seen up close, and the ground looked a long way down.

'We'll just get a few boxes and then nip into Mook-Don-Aldies, Johnny. It's just round the back there. I'll treat you to a large American coffee and a doughnut.'

What was he on about? Mook-Don-Aldies? Then the penny dropped. He meant McDonald's. Most French people refer to McDonald's as 'McDo' and they have generally embraced the hamburger chain with great gusto. They see it as the ultimate American experience and the drive-in restaurants are a big attraction. Serge clearly was no exception. But Mook-Don-Aldies? I'd never heard it called that.

I was beginning to wish I'd never agreed to come. Serge had roped in Diddy to help us and he was down below in front of the van listening to hip hop on his iPod. Serge was edging himself along the rim of the skip. 'I'm going down,' he said. 'I need to take a closer look at those boxes.'

I had a flash premonition of him falling and breaking his neck. I was imagining what Helen would say if she could see us now. I hadn't phoned her as I'd hoped this would only take a few minutes and I'd be home in time for dinner. Serge was lowering himself, hanging by his hands. There was a pile of boxes and broken sheets of polystyrene below and he let go and crunched into them, rolling over and sliding through until he hit the bottom of the skip.

'I'm down!' he yelled, delighted. His voice echoed in the metal box. There was a scrunching noise as he blundered about, and then a loud 'bong' followed by a string of curses.

'Hey, Johnny, you still there?'

'Yes, Serge,' I said, 'I'm still here.'

'I've found a couple of good ones. I'm going to pass them up to you. Get Diddy over here, he can help you.'

I looked down at the shadowy figure of Diddy. He was now leaning against the van, nodding his head in time to the beat, nonchalantly smoking a cigarette. He didn't give a damn. I shouted down to him. 'Your dad wants to know if you're coming up to help him!' He flicked a glowing cigarette stub into the dark in a shower of sparks. 'I'm going for more fags.'

I called down to Serge: 'He's going for cigarettes.'

'What? Tell him to wait a minute, just to get these boxes out.'

But it was too late. Diddy had jumped in the van, revved it up and driven off.

'What's going on? Was that the van?'

'Yes, he's gone,' I said.

'Gone?' He was astounded.

'He said he wouldn't be long.'

'He's a half-wit that boy,' groaned Serge. 'What am I going to do with him?'

It was cold and I'd had enough of this pantomime. I was remembering the times Serge had been hurt being called a 'half-wit' himself. I was ready for my promised American coffee and doughnut. 'Come on then pass them up,' I said, 'I can do this on my own.'

'They're a bit hard to manoeuvre Johnny, but I'll try.'

There was a scraping and the side of a cardboard box caught me in the face. I grabbed it and gave it a yank. It was a big one and the end was caught under the other boxes. I leant in to get a better hold, gave it a tug, then slipped and found myself rolling over the edge and falling down into the skip. I landed face down on a load of expanded polystyrene.

'Johnny, are you OK?' The voice was loud, right in my ear.

'I thought you wanted a *coup de main*,' I said, pretending I'd gone in to give him a helping hand rather than admit I'd fallen in. I looked up at the orange sky framed by the sides of the skip. 'Look, let's just get the boxes out and go for our coffee and doughnuts, eh?'

'Yes, fair enough, Johnny. Just lift the other side of this one and we'll push it out.'

I took one end of the flattened box and we pushed it up, trying to heft it over. But it didn't quite make it and fell back on us.

'If Diddy was up there he could pull it out,' said Serge irritably. He went to grab the other end of the box and let out a yell of pain.

'What's up?' I said. 'Are you OK?' He was bent over like a monkey.

'I think I've done my back in,' he said through clenched teeth. 'It's happened before.'

'Oh no!' I sympathised – it was the furniture dealer's nightmare, all too common.

'I always carry my belt with me, Johnny, for when my back goes, it's in the van.'

'Diddy'll be back in a bit,' I said. 'He can get it for you.'

'Where is he when I need him? He just doesn't seem to give a damn.'

'Oh, I think he does,' I reassured him, 'he's just young, that's all.' But my words had a hollow ring. Serge hobbled over to the side of the skip and tried to straighten up. He failed, gave a terrible moan and crouched down again.

'It's bad, Johnny,' he said looking sideways at me. 'I've really done it this time.'

'You'll be all right,' I said. 'Don't panic.'

'I'm not panicking, Johnny, I'm in pain.'

'I know,' I said. I was at a loss as to what to do. I reached up and grasped at the side of the skip. It was higher than I thought and the inside was smooth. I managed to hook my fingers over the top and pull my chin up to the rim, but I couldn't find a toehold and slipped back down again.

'Give Diddy a ring,' I said. 'Hurry him up. There's no way I can climb out without a leg up and with your back that's not an option.'

'Sorry, Johnny, but I left my phone in the van. I can't believe this has happened.'

'Don't worry, Serge, we'll be out of here soon.' I squatted down beside him. There was a chill in the air and I realised I'd left my mobile phone in my jacket in the van as well. I was just hoping Diddy wouldn't be long.

The *rocade* had gone quiet. Everyone was at home eating their suppers in front of the telly. That's where I'd have liked to have been. Helen would be worrying about where I was and I wished I'd rung her and told her where I was going. She would have advised me to come home and leave Serge to it and it would have been good advice in this case.

'What time is it?' Serge was bent over, leaning his bottom against the metal side of the skip. I pulled a polystyrene box over and sat down beside him and checked my watch. 'Just gone nine – Diddy will be back in a minute.'

'I hope so, Johnny. To be honest I wouldn't even trust him to put his trousers on.'

We sat listening. It was deathly quiet. Out in the country far from the centre of town most of the French seem to go to bed at nine and are up early with the birds. It was growing colder. Our breath was steaming and the chill was biting through my light windcheater.

'Feels like a frost's on its way,' said Serge. He looked a bit pathetic hunched over like that. 'How's the back?' I said.

He made an attempt to half stand and let out a squeal of pain. 'Not good. Even if Diddy comes back I don't know how I'll get out of here. You'll have to leave me for the binmen to take for recycling.' He gave an ironic laugh. 'I only wanted a couple of boxes, is that a lot to ask?'

'It'll be OK, we'll get you out,' I said. But as I thought about it, how exactly would we do that? I jumped up and down and slapped my arms against my sides. We were going to freeze in here.

'It's getting chilly,' said Serge. 'We could make a kind of little camp out of cardboard boxes to keep us warm, that's what *les clochards* do.'

I hesitated to ask him how he knew so much about what tramps do. But maybe it wasn't such a bad idea. I pulled one of the big flattened boxes over and tried to reassemble it. It kept collapsing but I managed to hold it together and wrap it round the pair of us. When I pulled the top flaps across it formed a little cardboard hut. It was slightly warmer inside and kept the cold air out.

'Thanks,' said Serge leaning in closer. 'We could pass the whole night here if we have to.'

'I bloody hope not!' I cried. I wasn't keen on spending the night in a cardboard box with Serge. He smelt strongly of tobacco and sweat, but it was definitely warmer in here and his body was giving off welcome heat. How did I get into these ridiculous situations with him? It was like he was jinxed.

'OK if I have a cigarette?' he asked.

'Well, no actually,' I said, feeling like a complete prig. 'I mean, you don't mind do you, Serge? Only I'll choke on the smoke in here.'

'But it might help ease the pain in my back, take my mind off it.' He sounded pathetic.

'Oh, all right,' I capitulated, 'but can you blow the smoke out of the box? They're a bit strong those Gitanes.'

He fumbled about and lit up, took a deep drag and let out a sigh of satisfaction. The classic aroma filled the box. I'd stopped smoking years ago but I was almost tempted to have one myself.

'How's it going with your move?' asked Serge. When I had told him about Farmer Fagot and how he was going to build a housing estate on the fields round our house he was shocked. 'I love your place,' he told me, 'it's so tranquil.'

'Helen's been searching for another property and we've put our house on the market,' I explained, 'but so far no luck.'

'Don't give up hope, something will turn up,' he said, blowing a couple of smoke rings and piercing them with his finger.

There was the sound of a vehicle driving slowly and pulling up alongside the skip.

'It's Diddy!' cried Serge, jumping up despite his bad back. He let out an agonising scream and dropped back down, moaning softly.

The van stopped, leaving its engine running. Then we heard it pulling away.

'What's he playing at?' said Serge. 'He's not driving off is he?'

I jumped up and banged on the metal side of the skip with my fist. The blows rang out like a deeply resonating bell. I put my hands up, grabbed the side of the skip again and pulled myself up to try to look over the edge, but it was no use – I couldn't get high enough. The van stopped, we heard the door slam and Diddy walking back, then putting his foot on the metal rungs and starting to climb. I looked up expectantly, waiting to see him appear but a stranger's face popped up. It was a man with cropped hair. He leant over, scanning the inside of the skip.

'Who's down there?' His voice was gruff and when he turned to the lamplight I saw he was wearing a dark jumper with a white line running across the chest.

Serge saw it too and hissed, *'Les flics, mon dieu!'*

'Is anyone down there?' The gendarme sounded irritable, like he wasn't a patient man. A torch beam swept the inside of the skip.

'What shall we do?' whispered Serge.

'We're not doing anything wrong,' I said, standing up. The torch shone in my face.

'Come out, you can't sleep in there!'

I emerged from the *clochard*-style cardboard box. It was obvious what the gendarme was thinking and I got an inkling of how illegal immigrants must feel when they are caught on the hop.

'We're not sleeping in here,' I said. 'We were looking for cardboard boxes and got stuck.' It sounded a bit lame.

'Stuck?' He sounded incredulous.

'Yes, my friend's hurt his back so he can't get out,' I said.

'Oh yes, where is your friend then?' asked the gendarme. He sounded like he thought I was making it up.

'Come on, show yourself,' I hissed at Serge, and kicked the box. It collapsed, revealing Serge bent over. He lifted one hand and tentatively gave the gendarme a little wave.

'*Bon-soir, M'sieu.*' His voice was weak and apologetic. 'My friend is telling the truth. I've hurt my back and can't get out.'

The gendarme looked unconvinced, like he imagined this might be some sort of a trap. He pulled back and we heard him climbing down the metal rungs. A car door opened and slammed again. We heard voices and the static and peeps of a two-way radio. Maybe he was calling for backup. Then came the scrape of boots on the metal rungs and two heads appeared over the edge of the skip.

'You say you've hurt your back?' It was our original gendarme.

'Yes, sir,' said Serge. 'I'm sorry. I don't know how it happened.'

'Could you climb out if we give you a hand?'

'I don't think so, sir, it's agonising. I think I've pulled a muscle.'

The second gendarme was on the tubby side and looked uncomfortable balanced up there. 'What about you?' He said looking at me. 'Have you hurt your back too?'

'No, sir,' I said, following Serge's obsequious example. 'I'm fine, just a bit cold.'

'What did you want cardboard boxes for?' said the one with cropped hair. 'Are you sleeping rough?'

'Oh no, sir,' Serge laughed like it was a ridiculous question. 'We're professional antiques dealers. We needed a big box to put a piece of furniture in.'

'It's for Eastern Europe,' I chipped in.

'So you're not sleeping rough then?'

'Oh no, sir!' said Serge. 'We live in houses.' That sounded a bit stupid, even to me, and I sniggered.

'What's so funny?' asked Cropped Hair.

'Nothing,' I said, feeling my face redden.

'Where's your house then?' Tubby asked me. 'You're a long way from home, aren't you?'

'I live not far away,' I said. 'In the Chalosse.'

'You're not from Belgium then?'

'No, I'm from England.'

'Oh yes, whereabouts?'

'London,' I said, 'originally.'

I was thinking about how long it seemed since we left London. It felt like a lifetime ago. Tubby said something to the other one. Then he nodded to us and they went back down. I didn't like the way this was going. I felt I was about to be arrested and deported back to England. They couldn't do that, could they? We were all in the EU. I hadn't done anything wrong.

We heard murmuring, scrapes on the ladder again and Tubby reappeared.

'Right, we're phoning *les pompiers*. They're used to climbing about like monkeys. Just relax, they'll be here directly.'

What a relief! I hopped from foot to foot. It was cold and the sooner the firemen arrived and got us out of here the better. When would I ever learn not to get involved in Serge's hare-brained schemes? I always ended up regretting it.

Serge was doubled up. His face was lit by the overhead neon lighting. He was clearly in considerable pain. I was beginning to feel sorry for him.

'I need a pee-pee Johnny,' he said pathetically.

'Can't you hang on a bit? We'll be out of here soon.'

'I'm desperate!'

'OK, we are in a skip,' I said. 'It'll be all right to go in here.'

'I'm scared,' he said, 'what with the gendarmes here.'

'They won't know. Just do it quietly.'

He waddled over to the other side in the shadows and there was the unmistakable sound of running water against the metal side of the iron box. It seemed to go on for ages. When he'd finished he let out a sigh of relief just in case there was any doubt about what he had been doing. In reality, in France men can pee anywhere and no one bats an eyelid. Helen and I were in a supermarket car park and a man relieved himself against the front of our car facing us while we sat there open-mouthed. Blokes stop anywhere and pass water like it's their God-given right.

The flattened cardboard bounced as Serge came back. 'I think I got away with it,' he whispered.

We heard sirens in the distance coming closer, then there was the flash of blue lights, and the sound of a heavy wagon arriving, raised voices, shouts and a general commotion. Two men wearing firemen's helmets appeared over the top edge of the skip.

'*Ça va?*' They were reassuringly calm and confident. An aluminium ladder was lowered and a fireman in blue overalls descended. I explained Serge had hurt his back but when he realised I was fine I was sent up and over the top to be guided down by the other one. He went back up and soon the pair of them reappeared, carefully lifting Serge over the edge and lowering him down to the ground. He stood bent over, gritting his teeth against the pain.

The *pompiers* and the gendarmes appeared to know one another and were shaking hands, chatting together, smiling and commenting on Serge's predicament.

'We're going to call an ambulance to take you to hospital,' said the tubby one.

Serge was mortified. 'No, not the hospital! I've got a special belt. My son has it in the van. I don't need to waste the rest of the evening hanging around there.' He was bent over looking up at the gendarme.

Tubby considered this for a moment, looking around for the phantom van.

'You're sure? You look pretty bad to me.'

Serge grasped his hand like a chimpanzee. 'I'll be fine, sir, honestly. As soon as I get my belt on, I'll be right as rain. My son will be here very soon.'

I could see a white van with its lights dipped slowly approaching. Diddy! He was back!

Serge had seen him too. He dropped the gendarme's hand, let out a cry and was off, shambling towards it, bent over like Quasimodo. I followed and soon caught up with him. Diddy seemed worried. He wound down the window and looked across at the police car.

'Where the hell have you been?' shouted Serge. He was livid. 'You idiot! Do you realise we've been trapped in that bloody tin box for hours? What were you playing at?

'I saw *les flics* and drove off,' he said. 'I thought they'd arrested you. You said never to talk to *les flics*. It's not my fault.'

Serge looked up at me and pulled an exasperated face. He opened the van door and felt around in the glove compartment.

'*Putain!* I was sure my belt was here. Well, never mind. We'd better just tell *les flics* we're off. They don't like it if you don't tell them what you're doing.'

The gendarmes and *pompiers* greeted him like a long-lost friend as he staggered back.

'Are you sure you're all right?' the tubby gendarme asked. 'We can still call the ambulance, get you up the hospital.'

'No, I'm fine, just a bit cold. My son's here now, we'll be OK.'

'We're all going up to McDo's for a coffee,' said Tubby. 'You're welcome to join us.' There was a roar of laughter from the *pompiers* and the other gendarme as they wandered towards McDonald's.

Serge looked up at me. 'We could go with them, Johnny,' he said. 'Why not? I'll buy you that coffee and doughnut I promised you.'

It didn't look like I was going to be able to get out of it. 'I'll just ring Helen,' I said, reaching into my coat pocket in the van and retrieving my mobile. 'She'll be worried.'

This, as it turned out, was an understatement. 'I've been worried sick,' she said as soon as she answered. 'Where are you?'

'I'm with the gendarmes and the *pompiers*,' I said. 'It's all right, I'm OK. Everyone's OK.'

'What! Are you with Serge?'

'We're just going to McDonald's for a coffee,' I explained. 'I've got to wait for Serge and Diddy to drop me back to my van and I can't really say no. I'll tell you all about it when I get home.'

'What on earth's happened? Oh, I give up – just come home soon.'

I followed the party up to the brightly lit entrance of McDonald's. I could hear the cropped-haired gendarme talking to Serge who was beside him, still bent over, walking with a monkey-like rolling gait.

'So what exactly are these Eastern Europeans buying then?' he was asking, bending down to speak to him. I heard Serge launching into an enthusiastic explanation.

And as we walked into McDonald's – gendarmes, *pompiers*, a man bent double – the young staff looked up briefly. And then carried on serving, totally unfazed.

9

STORKS AND BRIDGES

It was a warm Thursday afternoon and I was driving back to Dax with Serge after helping him deliver some furniture he had sold to a couple of newly-weds. The *brocante* markets were picking up after a cold winter and spring was in full bloom. The night of mayhem in the freezing skip was just a distant memory. I had agreed to give Serge a hand, but this time in just dropping off an art deco bedroom suite and armoire at a house on a small *lotissement* on the outskirts of Dax. 'It's not much stuff,' he explained, 'but it's difficult for me to lift on my own and Diddy's off chasing some big moneymaking scheme he reckons is going to earn him a fortune. He's too busy to help his poor old dad. Since the skip my back has been playing up. I have to remember to wear my belt even to lift light things.'

Young French couples tend to prefer stylish modern houses they have chosen from catalogues which they can have built to their own specifications on pleasant little estates. The *lotissement* was nice enough, but looking at all the houses squashed up together made me feel sick. This was what it would be like on the fields around our house. Helen was right, it would be unbearable – our beautiful natural countryside concreted over and ruined. She was out now viewing houses on her own. I had churlishly refused to go with her looking for a new place, pathetically trying to take a stand to stay in our old house, the one I realised I loved. Deep down I knew this sulking wouldn't work, but I would never admit to myself I was stubbornly fighting to make sure we never moved. When Helen took me to look at houses she thought were promising, I picked on any fault I could find. My task was made easier because restored houses in the Chalosse were too expensive and way beyond our budget. That coupled with the fact that the more people viewed our house and balked about the imminent housing estate, the more the price slipped down. It was a double-edged sword and a nightmare that I was trying to block out of my everyday life.

Serge and I were taking a shortcut down a narrow country road that crossed open fields and woodland between two small villages. In March, when the rains come, the River Adour bursts its banks and muddy water swirls through the bushes and brambles flooding the land here. When the floods recede you can see where the water has risen by the muddy line that runs along the bushes and up tree trunks.

Often, coming back late from markets on warm summer nights, I have stopped and gazed in wonder at the starry sky, listening to the owls and the scurrying of small night animals foraging in the hedgerows. These fields and small streams are home to many beavers, or *castors* as the French call them. I'm not sure that these *castors* aren't actually coypu, the South American beaver-like rodent, but whatever they are the place is teeming with them. Whenever Helen and I take this route we say we are going via 'Beaverland' and we have often had to swerve to avoid them. Not everyone is so careful, however, and these large rodents often appear as bloodied roadkill.

The beavers are not the only wildlife that treats this swathe of untamed countryside as home. Every year several pairs of storks return to their nests in the trees that run alongside the river to raise new broods. Someone in the nearby village of St-Vincent-de-Paul erected a wooden platform on a pole in their garden to entice the storks to build a nest there, and every year their efforts were rewarded by the return of a pair of storks raising their chicks high up above their garden. It was a regular attraction for motorists passing through. When they sold the house the new owners, with amazing insensitivity, cut down the pole and the storks, whose nest they had destroyed, rejoined the others nesting in the trees alongside the riverbank nearby. Since then, passing locals regularly sound their horns loudly to express their disapproval.

Serge was laughing in disbelief at the muddy lines along the bushes and trees, marvelling at how high the waters had risen over the winter.

'Heh! Look at that,' said Serge, pointing at the body of a dead *castor* slumped by the roadside. 'He's a big one.'

He was too. And he had a thin, rat-like tail. That was definitely a coypu. The size of them was shocking – it was like a small terrier. It was hard to believe that such giant rodents were living here in south-west France. There had been a scare when a local fisherman contracted Weil's disease, a dangerous virus which can be spread by rodents' urine infecting the river water. The coypu was thought to be the obvious culprit and poison had been laid in an attempt to wipe them out. But they had continued to thrive over the winter months, safe in their own watery domain. Now the cars and lorries had returned they were falling casualty to the passing traffic.

Ahead was the narrow bridge that crossed the River Adour. It is long and narrow and cars intending to cross are guided by two arrows, one red and one white, which indicate who has the right of way. I often find it difficult to tell which is which, and I'm sure I'm not the only one. I normally follow the rule that if someone is already on the other end of the bridge I wait for them to come through.

'There's a hold-up on the bridge,' said Serge. '*Putain!* It's stretching back both sides.'

'Probably an accident,' I said.

We pulled up. There were about ten cars ahead of us. Doors were opened and drivers were climbing out to see what was happening. We sat back and waited for the traffic to start moving.

'I meant to ask you, Johnny,' said Serge, lighting up one of his Gitanes cigarettes. 'You told me once that you put a new roof on your house when you first bought it.'

'Well, yes, I did, but I know very little about roofing. We had an English builder staying with us, and we did it together.'

'I thought you had, only I was going to ask if you would help me strip down an old roof and retile it. You could show me how it's done.'

I wasn't really a builder and tiling a roof was a big commitment. Could I afford the time? 'I thought you lived in a flat, Serge,' I said.

'No, it's not my roof, Johnny. Someone has asked me to reroof a house for them, that's all. I thought you might want to help me.'

'Well, I'm not sure if I can,' I said, playing for time. Alarm bells were ringing in my head. 'I'm not sure if I'm up to it. It was a while ago and I don't know if I can remember how to do it.'

'I bet you can. I would be really grateful if you could give me a hand.'

'What's this all about?' I said. I had a feeling there was more to this than he was letting on. His voice had a pleading edge to it.

'OK, Johnny, if you really want to know, I'm in a bit of a tight corner. You remember that guy, the one with the beautiful walnut buffet with the woodworm in it?'

'The thug who was going to have you fed to the pigs or cemented into a Spanish motorway?'

'Well, not exactly. But yes, that's the one.'

'The Romanian with the flash flat in Biarritz?'

'Yes, him. He wasn't too pleased about not getting his buffet back. I said we'd had a few problems but he's not a very patient man. He got very irritated and as I didn't have enough to pay him for the buffet he offered me some other options.'

'What sort of options?' I asked.

'Some of them were non-starters really. You're not far off with that "being fed to the pigs" one. It was actually mentioned.'

'You didn't fancy that then?' I said, laughing.

'Not really, Johnny, no,' he said, deadly serious. 'But he assured me that if I could fix the roof for a friend of his he would maybe forget about the buffet.'

'What, only maybe?' I said.

'Well, what choice have I got? I don't really want to get killed or worse.'

'What could be worse?'

'Believe me, there are a lot of things worse!'

'I suppose there probably are.'

'*Mais oui*, those guys can be very imaginative. Best not to think about it, eh? This house he wants me to reroof is in the foothills of the Pyrenees. It's a very nice Basque house.'

'Crikey! They're usually really big.'

'So, can you help me out?' he begged. 'If you could just show me how it's done – the basics, so to speak – I'm sure I can finish it myself. That's as long as my back holds out.'

I felt sorry for him when he mentioned his back and caved in. 'Well, all right Serge, but will Diddy be helping, labouring or something? After all, he got you into this.'

'No, he's refusing to help... not his thing, apparently. And he made the excuse that he has to see his little daughter at weekends, but it's not true, he hardly ever bothers. I want to start it next week. The guy has a short fuse. I don't want to try his patience any more than I have done already.'

I suppose if it stopped him being fed to the pigs it wasn't that much to ask. But I knew from experience that reroofing could be a big job. I was kicking myself for being such a soft touch.

Serge flicked the burning stub of his cigarette onto the road and ground it out with his boot. 'This is *pénible*! Are we going to have to wait here all day?'

There was a Gateau pulled up in front of us. The Gateau is a make of small car that can be driven without a licence, and they tend to be owned by either retired peasants or drunk drivers who have been banned from a more powerful vehicle. This one was driven by a little old man wearing a tweed jacket and beret. He was sitting, patiently waiting, gripping the steering wheel with both hands. When Serge rapped on his window he jumped.

'What's going on, *chef*?' Serge asked.

The little man turned with a frightened look on his face and slid open the window. 'I think there's a problem on the bridge, *m'sieu*.'

'Well, I can see that. But what sort of problem?'

'I don't know, *m'sieu*.' He slid his window shut and turned and faced the front.

Serge looked heavenward and sighed. 'Come on, I'm going to see what's up.' We strolled over and joined a small crowd that had gathered by the bridge. Looking upriver I could see the storks' nests high up at the top of the trees. A large stork was perched on one of them and there were two young storks craning their necks, eager for food.

In the middle of the bridge two cars had pulled up, facing one another. The one coming from the other side was a big shiny white Mercedes saloon. It looked like the two drivers had set off from either side at the same time and met in the middle. The driver on our side clearly had right of way. It was a stand-off.

'The *connard* in the Mercedes is refusing to budge,' said a man in blue overalls. 'I'm late for an important appointment.'

'Why won't he back up?' I asked. 'If he doesn't, we'll be here all night.'

'You're right,' said Blue Overalls. 'I always take this shortcut to save time. If this happens, what's the point?'

Serge was looking over at the Mercedes. His face drained of colour, and when he looked at me I could see panic in his eyes.

Someone sounded their horn behind us and this set off a chorus of high-pitched hooting. Serge turned to the man in blue overalls.

'Come on, let's be sensible here. If you start to back up, we'll do the same and everyone can go home.'

'You're joking,' said the man. 'It's my right of way. I'm not going to back up for you or anyone else.'

'Someone's got to see sense,' said Serge. 'You're acting like a kid.'

'Don't call me a kid, friend. It's him in the flash car that's the kid. Tell him to back up.'

'Look, let's surprise everyone,' said Serge. 'We've all got things to do. This is how wars start.'

Blue Overalls looked at Serge, then turned to me. 'What do you think?' he asked.

'Don't ask him, he's English,' said Serge. 'The English never back down, they're maniacs.'

'We are not,' I said, deciding that I wasn't going to take that kind of slur.

'You went into Iraq with the Americans. Blair was Bush's poodle, everyone knows that,' said Serge.

'OK he was, I admit that. But...' I was lost now. I didn't have an acceptable come back.

'All right, I'll back up,' said Blue Overalls resignedly. 'I'm convinced – this is stupid.'

He climbed into his car and began to reverse as Serge directed the traffic behind, waving his hands, cajoling the drivers. Gradually the line moved back until the way was clear for the cars on the bridge to back off, leaving an open road for the Mercedes. The big white saloon came rolling over and pulled up alongside us. The window was wound down and I found I was looking into the sneering face of Bruno the Basque.

'Eh, Rosbif! Long time no see.' He reached out to shake my hand, grinning like he was my old pal. I looked at Serge. He seemed cowed, not at all like his usual self.

'I'm still waiting, Serge,' said Bruno, frowning. 'I hope you're not going to let me down.'

Serge had a forced grin on his face. 'Don't worry, Bruno, I'm coming next week. And Johnny here, he's an expert; he's agreed to help me.'

Bruno turned to me, smiling. 'Hey, I'm impressed! And good, I'm glad you'll be there, Rosbif, to make sure he doesn't mess things up.' He made a dismissive gesture, the window rolled up and the Mercedes accelerated off.

As we walked back to our van I tackled Serge. 'What was all that about then?'

'What's that, Johnny?'

'I thought Bruno was your sworn enemy.'

'No, that's not true, we went to school together.'

'Come on, Serge, last time I saw you two together you were rolling on the floor pulling each other's hair out.'

'Yes, well things have changed since then, Johnny. Old friends can always make up. We've got a bond, Bruno and me.'

I didn't believe a word of it. I wasn't as green as I had been when I first met Serge and started working the markets. I remembered he had said it was Bruno who put him onto the Romanian with the walnut buffet at Biarritz. That was the key to his fawning manner with Bruno. Serge was frightened and the pair of them had him running scared.

'So it's Bruno's roof we'll be fixing next week?' I said.

'It's one of his properties, yes.' He opened the van door and stopped.

'Look, I know what you think of me, but I didn't have much choice here. That Romanian and Bruno have been threatening me for months. Now they've agreed that if I do this, I'll be quits and all that business with the buffet will be behind me.' He climbed in and we drove off.

'You're right, though, it was Diddy's fault anyway,' he moaned as we crossed the bridge, which was now clear and back to normal.

We drove through the village and when we passed the front garden where the storks' nest used to be Serge sounded his horn in protest. We could hear the chorus of hoots behind us as we headed back to the market.

10

EAGLES AND SNOWY MOUNTAINS

Sitting up high on a roof looking out across open countryside, breathing in fresh, clean air with the rest of the world stretched out below you – there's nothing quite like it. The blue-grey shadow of the Pyrenees dominated the skyline. A filmy mist hung over the secret valleys and foothills that rolled up to where the mountains began their push skywards.

Serge was sitting on the tiles beside me with a faraway look in his eyes. When he turned and saw me looking at him he gave me a warm smile. This was the happiest I'd seen him since he had returned from Martinique, a broken man. We were perched side by side three storeys up on the roof of a big house with *Basque rouge* (dark red) shutters and doors. I had agreed to help him strip the roof, fix any beams that were damaged and re-batten and retile it. I was slowly adjusting to looking down from that height. After a while, looking down becomes as normal as looking up. When I was seven a bigger boy used to ambush me on my way home from junior school. He would wrestle me to the ground and sit on my chest, pinning me down by my wrists and dribbling spit on my face. It made my life a misery. I couldn't beat him, he was much stronger than me, so I devised a plan: I rushed out of school as soon as class was over and climbed as high as possible up a big old oak tree. I was safe up there in the tree and I discovered that no one ever looked up so no one knew I was there. From my vantage point I watched the bully boy pass on his way home.

Gazing at the towering snow-capped mountains of the Pyrenees I was thinking about how my life had completely changed since we moved to France. There was still this excitement bubbling away. It was strange but I felt that if I pinched myself I might wake up and it would have all been a dream. I had a sense of wonder that never quite went away. However familiar our life became here, there was always that underlying thrill. It wasn't going to suddenly end. We didn't have to pack up and go home. We weren't on holiday. This was our life. It was real: these mountains, this beautiful countryside, the balmy air, the sunshine.

'Look, Johnny, eagles!' Serge was on his feet. Circling in the distance were the silhouettes of two large birds of prey. Even from here you could see the distinctive way the wing feathers splayed out as they rose on the thermals. They were magnificent! And there was a third joining them. Higher and higher, soaring effortlessly in the blue sky.

Eagles! *Aigles!* The word sounds the same in French as in English. They are the stuff of legends, the unchallenged rulers of the bird kingdom. Nothing can touch them. The sight of them sets the pulse racing. The idea that they nest high up on unreachable eyries in the mountains adds to their mystery.

'*L'aigle royal!*' Serge cried. 'The most beautiful eagle of all.'

I had seen these impressive birds before, but only when driving through the Pyrenees on the way to Spain. To see them here in the foothills was thrilling.

'We call them golden eagles in English,' I said, 'but I think the word royal is better.'

'It's true, they are royal,' said Serge, 'the king of all the birds.'

We watched them circling, fascinated. I hoped they might come even nearer, but they eventually soared off and away, heading back to the mountains.

We sat back down side by side, and contemplated the breathtaking view.

Serge broke the silence. 'Well, what do you think, Johnny? Will we be able to do it, you know, just the two of us?'

'Oh, the roof you mean? It's going to be quite a job,' I said. 'I hadn't expected such a big house.'

'I didn't have much choice, Johnny. Bruno told me he only just managed to persuade that Romanian thug from Biarritz to give me another chance. If it hadn't been for Bruno, who knows what would have happened?'

This sounded familiar. Serge was being bullied – like I was as a kid – by the Romanian and, I was certain, by Bruno, who was also a conman. I felt sorry for Serge.

'Better get started then,' I said. I didn't believe that Bruno was on his side and nothing Serge said was going to convince me.

'You're the boss,' said Serge. 'I'm being guided by you here.'

This was a turnaround. It was Serge who had shown me the ropes when I first started out as a *brocanteur*. Now he was putting his faith in my building skills. I wanted to remind him that I had only ever done one roof before and that was when I had helped Tony, a friend of ours who was a skilled builder and carpenter. But I decided to shut up about that. It was hard to believe but maybe Serge would be willing to take advice from me for a change.

'We'll start by stripping off all these old tiles,' I said, prising up a pair of broken ones and lobbing them into the air. They curved and fell, hitting the ground below with a satisfying shattering sound.

'Ooh, I like that,' said Serge, yanking up some more. 'I always liked breaking things when I was a lad.' He slung the tiles over the edge and began on another row. Within a couple of hours we had stripped back a quarter of the roof and the resulting debris was spread round the back of the house like a bomb had hit it. We stopped for a breather and Serge lit up one of his strong cigarettes.

Now that we had revealed the support beams I could see places where we were going to have to carry out repairs. I fetched a big steel jemmy I had bought when I was working with Tony and set about wrenching apart a joint between two beams that needed replacing.

As I worked I began humming to myself the old Drifters' song 'Up on the Roof', and was surprised when Serge joined in on the chorus, singing out the 'up on the roof' bits in English. We worked away, singing together, levering off broken beams and slinging the bits over the edge.

'*Putain!* These are full of wormholes,' said Serge.

'Well, they've been here a few hundred years, it's hardly surprising,' I said. He was right, though; they were like honeycomb on the surface. But once you drilled down through the woodwormy bit the centres were as solid as iron. I'd broken several drill bits on ancient oak beams like this in our home when Helen wanted something hung up.

We fetched a fresh piece of oak, sawed it to size and nailed it into place, strengthening the roof. Below us was the old *grenier* (loft). I nipped down the ladder to fetch another replacement length of wood from the van and when I came back up with it Serge had disappeared. I shouted out for him but there was no reply. What was he playing at? I yelled for him again and heard an answering shout from somewhere way down below inside the house. I swung down on a beam and landed with a thump on my feet in the *grenier*. The only light in here came from the gap in the roof and I could see a door made of planks at the far end. I opened it and felt my way down a narrow wooden staircase to the floor below. It was a long dark hallway. I called to Serge again. Nothing. At the end of the passage I could see a soft glow of light. I walked towards it and entered a furnished bedroom with one shutter half open letting in the daylight. There was a heavy carved walnut double bed with two *chevets* and an armoire. I had the feeling the old owner could walk in any minute. A chill ran through me when I heard a thundering noise coming up a wooden staircase. Then Serge appeared, clumping along the hall.

'What's up, Johnny?' He was carrying an old brass candlestick and puffing from the exertion.

'I wondered where you were,' I said.

'Not scared are you – of ghosts, perhaps?'

'No,' I said quickly, then changed the subject. 'Where were you?'

'I was just having a look around.'

'So I see,' I said. 'Whose house is this?'

'I don't know but apparently the guy died recently. I think the Romanian bought it. He wants it fixed up so he can sell it for a good price.'

He placed the candlestick on the floor and walked over to one of the *chevets*. He pulled out the drawer, reached in and removed a white china potty, which he pushed under the bed. Then he felt around in the space where the drawer had been, tipped the *chevet* on its side and shook it about vigorously.

There was the sound of something dropping and a piece of chocolate money, the sort I used to get given at Christmas when I was a kid with a gold paper wrapper on the outside, fell, spun and rolled across the wooden floor, landing at my feet. Serge let out a cry of triumph. I bent down and picked it up. It felt harder than I had imagined... and heavier.

Serge was beaming. 'There you are, Johnny, what do you think?'

I examined it more closely. This wasn't chocolate money. I was disappointed. I just fancied a piece of chocolate, although it might have been a bit old. But it couldn't be what it looked like, could it?

'It says it's a Mexican fifty pesos,' I said. 'It can't be real gold, can it?'

Serge ignored me. He was back shaking the *chevet* again. There were two clunks, and two more coins fell out. He was ecstatic.

'I've hit the jackpot, Johnny! Who would have thought it? I knew my luck would change one day and today's the day!' He did a little dance, holding the coins aloft and waving them above his head.

'Just a minute, Serge,' I said. 'If they are gold, you can't keep these. What if the Romanian knows they're there?'

'Listen,' said Serge, 'have you ever wondered why when you buy these *chevets* at auction or in house sales the inside alabaster linings are dislodged or broken?'

Now he came to mention it, he was right. Normally the little cupboards in these bedside tables were lined with marble or alabaster to make it easier to clean them when the potty that was kept inside slopped its contents. I've had English people who have bought these *chevets* ask me, 'This is where they kept their jug of drinking water to keep it cool, was it?' I usually don't bother to enlighten them, and just say, 'Oh, yes!' Best not to gross out a prospective customer. But I had noticed that the insides were often damaged.

'Every *brocanteur* knows that country folk don't trust banks and they don't want the taxman to get their hands on their hard-earned cash,' said Serge. 'So they hide money away under the mattress or purchase valuable gold coins that go up in value and can be turned into cash for a rainy day. The first thing relatives or dealers do when someone dies is break up the insides of these *chevets* and search for anything hidden down behind the drawers. It's a well-known fact. People have been murdered for less.'

This was true. I had heard that when Gaston, the old peasant farmer who owned our house, died, a bunch of local lads had broken into the house and ransacked it looking for any hidden Louis d'or coins.

'I know about gold, Johnny, and these coins are worth a small fortune.'

'Are you mad? You can't take them,' I insisted, 'it's theft. They belong to the owner – that bloke who wants your guts for garters. Don't take any more risks, Serge.'

'Don't worry, Johnny, this furniture isn't his – it's mine. We have already come to an arrangement about it.'

'How do you mean "come to an arrangement"?'

'Bruno said I can take the furniture as payment for doing the roof.'

So that was what this was all about? The penny dropped. Lord Snooty was right – Serge the Snurge. He had pulled a fast one on me yet again. I thought his life was in danger, but in reality he'd negotiated doing a house clearance on the back of my helping him do the roof. What a sucker I was!

He was biting the fifty peso pieces now, examining them, shining them on the seat of his trousers. Suddenly it tickled me and I found myself laughing. I couldn't be mad at him for long. He was back on form again. He may have been a 'snurge' but he was the Serge the Snurge I knew and loved. I was relieved he had avoided any comeback for destroying the beautiful walnut buffet. And basically I liked the guy. It was great he had found the gold coins. God knows he needed some good news and I was sure he could do with the money.

'They're valuable then, are they?' I asked, wreathed in smiles.

'Listen, Johnny, I really do know what I'm talking about. You have to if you're doing *achat d'or*, or you end up losing out. These gold Mexican fifty Peso pieces are the business! They call them "poor man's gold". I can't say exactly how much they're worth today... but it's a lot.'

'So the poor bloke who slept in this bed and just died missed out on spending them?' I said.

'It happens. Life can be hard sometimes... and so can death.'

He spun one of the coins in the air, caught it and whacked it on the back of his hand. He looked at me questioningly...

'Heads!' I said.

He lifted his hand to reveal it was 'tails', the figure of an angel holding a wreath in the air.

'Bad luck, Johnny. Better luck next time, eh?' He laughed, gave me a hug and slipped the coins into his pocket.

There was a shout from down below and we stopped for a moment, listening. Then it came again, a gruff voice bellowing out for Serge.

'Sounds like someone's calling you,' I said.

Serge looked guilty and his hand went to his pocket as if to protect his stash of gold coins.

The voice yelled again. Serge froze. 'It's Bruno!' He looked scared.

'Better go and see what he wants,' I said. Serge didn't move.

'He knows we're here,' I said. 'Your van's outside and there are broken tiles everywhere.'

Serge pulled a cartoon face of doom and I followed him back along the hallway, and up into the *grenier*.

'Bend down so I can climb on your back and reach the beams,' he said.

Reluctantly I knelt down and he clambered over me, stepping on my shoulders and squashing my ear painfully as he pulled himself up. Once back on the roof he reached down and tried to pull me up after him. I hung for a moment with my legs pedalling in the air until he lost his grip. I landed heavily on the wooden planks of the *grenier* floor, lost my balance and fell over.

'Find something to stand on,' said Serge. 'I can't pull you up all the way.'

I searched around the *grenier* and found a dusty rush-seated chair. When I stood on it my foot went right through the straw.

Bruno bellowed out for Serge again. 'It's no good, Johnny, you'll have to go down the stairs and out the front door. I'll climb down the ladder and see what he wants.'

'Right,' I said, and set off down the wooden stairs and along the dark hallway until I reached the winding staircase that led to the entrance hall and front door. The heavy oak door was locked fast and I slid back the series of iron bolts. It swung back with a loud creak. I walked out into the bright sunlight and looked across to where Bruno was standing with one foot on the bottom rung of the ladder. He was glowering up at Serge, who was coming down cautiously. When he reached the ground Bruno stepped back and Serge turned to face him. He was grinning like a chimp, more in fear than good humour.

'What's all this?' said Bruno, gesturing at the broken tiles strewn on the ground. He looked annoyed. 'I hope you're going to clear up all this mess.'

'Don't worry, Bruno, we will,' said Serge. 'We've got to get all the old tiles off first, it's the only way.'

Bruno turned to me. 'Is this right, you've got to just throw this stuff about?'

'Well, yes, we'll make a start shovelling it up tonight,' I assured him.

'It's really hard work this is,' said Serge. He pulled his spotted handkerchief out of his pocket and mopped his brow to emphasise the point and I saw something glittering fly out, curve in the air, and roll in the grass. Serge saw it too and his eyebrows went up in disbelief. It was one of the gold coins! Without a second thought I stepped forward and put my foot on it. I coughed and tried to look nonchalant. Had Bruno noticed?

Serge went into action. He took Bruno's arm and guided him away, pointing up at the roof and explaining what we were doing. Bruno shook him off and my heart sank as he came striding back to me. He stopped and stared into my eyes. I stared back, trying to keep my cool. I was certain he had seen me step on the coin, which now felt like it was red hot under my foot. I waited in dread, holding my breath. Then, suddenly, Bruno gave me a big grin and shook my hand, holding on tight.

'Good... good,' he said, 'keep up the work, John, and don't let this joker sit down on the job, eh? Anything to do with hard work – he hates it.' He pulled me in closer and I felt my flesh crawl. I was sure he had seen the gold coin and was just playing with me.

'Oh, he's slaving away,' I blurted out, 'can't stop him.' I glanced at Serge, who threw me a tight grin.

'The guy who's bought this is *un gros bonnet*,' (a big cheese) said Bruno. 'I don't want a rushed job, but the sooner you can get it done the better.'

'We'll do our best,' said Serge, 'you can trust me, *copain*.'

Bruno flinched when Serge called him *copain*. I didn't think Serge was his mate any longer – more like his slave. He turned on his heel, strode over to his white Merc and drove off, bumping over the broken tiles. I wiped my hand on my jeans and it wasn't till he was completely out of sight that I had the nerve to bend down and retrieve the gold coin. I handed it to Serge.

'Thanks, Johnny,' he said. 'I was nearly a goner then. That was quick thinking.'

'Couldn't let Bruno get your gold, could we?' I said.

'Too right! Let's call it a day, eh?'

'Yeah, let's,' I said. My confrontation with Bruno had left me shaken.

'And remember, best not to mention this gold business to anyone. You know what people are like. If it ever got back to Bruno, or the *gros bonnet*, I'm a dead man.'

'Don't worry, Serge,' I said, 'my lips are sealed.'

'Good, Johnny, I knew I could trust you. A couple more days like this and I'll have got the hang of this roofing lark. I'll get Diddy to help me finish off the job.'

'OK. Serge,' I said, 'are you sure?' I couldn't believe I would be off the hook so soon.

'*Mais oui*, Johnny, I don't want to take over your life.'

Don't you? I thought. He was wrapping the coins up carefully in his spotted hankie and his eyes were glinting. I couldn't help noticing that he had begun to look a bit like Fagin.

11

TO THE WOODS

It was like a scene out of the old Wild West. We had drawn up our vehicles and formed protective circles. The *brocanteurs* – a motley crew so far – were installed over here: and over there, camped up in a clearing beyond the trees, were the *gitans*, their smart white vans, caravans and satellite dishes sparkling in the late-afternoon sunlight.

Meanwhile, the market traders, in an assortment of expensive camper vans and battered lorries, were gathered together in their camp, chatting and shooting the breeze. Lining the woodland tracks were miscellaneous traders, erecting their stands and unloading their wares.

This was a weird and wonderful place to hold a market, a secret sylvan world deep in the Landes forest normally only inhabited by deer and wild pigs.

Other dealers had told me about this El Dorado of fairs; a huge market held in the depth of the woods. In previous years they had offered this as an excuse as to why there was nobody at whatever town market we were doing.

'They've all gone to the big fair in the forest,' they'd say wistfully, and I'd wished I was there, wherever that was. They might as well have been talking about the Teddy Bears' Picnic. Serge had suggested we do it this year. He'd said it would be all of us together, like before his break-up with Angelique. I didn't like to point out to him that he was on his own now and so it wouldn't be quite the same, but he insisted we hurry up and book a pitch at this fabled market, which he said was at a place called Ousse-Suzan.

'Helen, you must book it tomorrow.' He was adamant. 'Only a few *brocanteurs* will be there, just those in the know.' He described it like he was a member of an elite clan. 'The place is always packed with people. They get over twenty thousand visitors in just the one day, it's unbelievable.' He had scribbled down a contact number before he left and Helen booked us a pitch.

And now here we were in this impressive forest, surrounded by lofty pines in the heart of Gascony. It was only a forty-minute drive from our house in the Chalosse but the landscape was completely different.

We had turned up earlier in the afternoon and joined the queue of white vans stretching back along the forest roads, waiting to be checked into our respective places by an army of men in Day-Glo jackets. Following the line of vehicles bumping along the sandy tracks through the trees we had marvelled at how fantastic the forest was with the sun shining down through the pines. It was thrilling to think we were going to be camped out here for the night. This job wasn't like work at all. The market would start the next day so we had time to meander around and gawp at all the other dealers and peruse their stands. I told Helen I was going for a wander and as I ambled past the rest of the bric-a-brac and antique dealers I couldn't help but notice that us *brocanteurs* were less of an elite clan than a hodgepodge of raggle-taggle miscreants. I was looking out for Serge and Diddy but there was no sign of them.

Someone tapped me on the shoulder. I turned, but there was no one there.

'If you go down to the woods today, you better not go alone.'

I swung round the other way and saw Reg had ducked down. 'Oi, oi! John, what brings you to this neck of the woods?' He had a manic grin on his face like Jack Nicholson in *The Shining*. But the real shock was that his bushy Rolling Stones hairstyle had gone. His head was now shorn very short, right down to the scalp! I must have looked surprised because he chuckled, stood up and rubbed his head.

'Decided to change me image. I've not been inside, if that's what you're thinking.'

'No, I wasn't,' I said, embarrassed. What I had been thinking was he looked terrifying without hair. Like some kind of axe murderer. Also, he had tattoos on his earlobes that I hadn't noticed before.

'And I haven't got nits, neither.'

'It never crossed my mind,' I said. 'It's good, it suits you,' I lied.

'Can't go on livin' in the sixties forever, can you?'

'Why not?' I joked.

'Yeah, well, that'd be good, but it ain't gonna happen, is it? First time you been here?' he asked, changing the subject.

'We thought we'd see what it was like,' I said. 'Serge insisted we should book in and do it.'

'You always do what he says then, do you?'

'No, not exactly.' I felt my face redden. I was finding it difficult to come to terms with how violent he looked.

'I heard about what happened to old Sergey with that Angelique sort,' said Reg. 'She was a right little darlin', wasn't she? And he was batting well above his average there. It had to happen.' He put his arm round my shoulders. 'Actually, John, this market is usually a good one. Punters galore! You hardly get a chance to think once they start pouring in. Me and Rita have got our caravan parked just over there, but I'll move over to join you lot. We can get together later for a drink and a bit of a laugh. Keep the old Brit spirit alive. What do you say?'

I looked across and could see his van and battered caravan. And there was Rita, lounging out front on a plastic recliner, smoking a fag. She saw me and waved. I waved back. 'Right then,' I said. 'You're on. I'm just taking a stroll, see what's happening.'

'Yeah, all right mate, see you later,' he said, patting me on the back.

I liked Reg. I knew a lot of the French dealers were wary of him, but his heart was in the right place, even if he wasn't much moved by Serge's little tragedy. I'd mixed with a few characters like him when I was a musician and also working in the music business. He was a maniac, but he was one of our maniacs.

I set off through the trees, idly looking at the stands being set up ready for the early morning start. Produce by local farmers and work by artisans from the Landes region appeared to be a strong theme. There were woven baskets, wooden clogs, regional pottery, home-made bonbons, wines, cheeses, foie gras, and all types of foodstuffs. Also the inevitable stall selling cooked preserved meat sausages made from every minced-up animal imaginable: pig, cow, rabbit, goose, wild boar, deer, horse... you name it. I was surprised to see they even had sausages made from donkey flesh. I couldn't imagine that being a particularly popular line, although there's no accounting for taste. The French rule is 'if it moves, eat it'. As vegetarians we were appalled. At least they hadn't got round to selling kitten or puppy sausages yet.

I was moving away feeling slightly queasy when I spotted Lord Snooty. He was bent over the counter of a nearby stand examining something, and as I drew closer I could see it was a display of vicious-looking pocket and sheath knives. They always draw men to them like flies. He was appraising a lethal-looking hunting knife. He wasn't wearing his deerstalker today, although he was still sporting a ridiculous pair of plus fours. He drew the knife from its sheath and made several stabbing motions with it.

'How's it going?' he said, wringing my hand. 'Great to see you, old boy.'

'Not bad,' I said. 'How about you?' I was leaning away in case he suddenly took it upon himself to try the knife out on me.

'Not so good. I'm very down at the moment. The markets have plunged to a new low and my sex life's taken a dive as well.'

I wasn't sure I really wanted to hear about his sex life. I noticed he stood quite close when he talked to me – making me feel a little uncomfortable.

'Oh, right,' I said, hoping he wouldn't elaborate further.

'Oh yah, I'm dead down there,' he said, pointing at his plus fours.

'Really?' I didn't want to know.

'I've got an English lady friend but in the bedroom we're all washed up.'

Erk! Too much information! But he was in full flow.

'Yes, totally dead. I really want to get a French girlfriend. I've been romantically involved with French women before and they are amazing! Really sensual, what.'

'Is that right?' I said.

'Oh yah, the French are famous for it. They believe sex is like eating, to be savoured and enjoyed.'

'Right.'

'My very first sexual experience was with an older French woman when I was a teenager on holiday. Fantastic!'

OK. So now he was getting my interest slightly.

'Yah, she introduced me to the delights of the boudoir. I've never forgotten it. Those first sexual experiences are always so exciting, aren't they? Like an illegal drug. I'm always looking for the excitement of that first high. Women have been my undoing throughout my life, old chap,' he went on. 'They're like beings from another planet, aren't they? Unfathomable!'

He was still holding the vicious-looking hunting knife in one hand, waving it about for emphasis. 'I've been involved with some beautiful women in my time. I was married to a beauty queen for a while but she tried to stab me, God knows why.' He made a jabbing movement with the knife and I stepped back in fear of being stabbed myself.

'But now my love life is all over; I'm finished, washed up. I'm not interested in sex any more.'

Two gypsy girls in their early teens wearing high heels, skintight white jeans and midriff-revealing tops tottered past. They were young and nubile with long, dark hair pulled up in flamboyant ponytails. We watched them, totally hypnotised. Algie had his mouth open. He was like a wolf poised for the kill.

'Jailbait,' I said matter-of-factly.

The irony of what he had just said about not being interested in sex any more hit him and he burst into uproarious laughter, falling about, hysterical, holding onto my arm.

We looked back at the girls. They had stopped and were being chatted up by a flash, shaven-headed young dude in hip-hop gear. Their body language indicated they fancied him like mad and thought he was pretty cool.

Algie was still chortling to himself, and as I gazed at the trio I realised I knew the young dude. Yes, there could be no doubt about it... it was Diddy! He was on the case: schmoozing, preening, leering, lascivious – giving them the works.

'Yeah, go for it, laddie!' yelled Algie. 'Give them one for me!'

I found this outburst amusing. Algie didn't give a damn. He was totally off the wall.

But our reveries were rudely interrupted by a piercing scream. A big, fat woman dressed all in black shoved past us, screeching and shaking her fist at Diddy. We watched, gobsmacked, as she tried to manhandle the girls from his over-amorous clutches. They pulled back, desperate to stay with the object of their desire. There were certainly no other likely lads about to lead them astray, just us ageing 'has-beens' and assorted bored husbands. Not much to choose from.

Diddy laughed in the face of the old woman, who cursed him venomously. At least, I assumed they were curses – I couldn't understand a word of what she was yelling.

'Oh, sweet days of youth!' said Algie. 'That's the sort of old crone those girls will turn into, just like their mother.'

'Grab it now while you still can!' he shouted through cupped hands.

'That's Diddy, Serge's son,' I said. The old woman was dragging the girls off and they were still waving at Diddy, desperately trying to communicate secret messages for a later liaison, no doubt. 'No!' said Algie. 'What, that reprobate Serge Bastarde's son? *C'est pas vrai!*'

'Yes, he's the son Serge didn't even know he had.'

'Well, I'll say this for him – the apple doesn't fall far from the tree.' He gave a loud guffaw.

12

FATHERS AND SONS

It was still dark when I woke early the next morning to the sound of voices and van doors slamming. We hadn't got to bed till two. When Serge arrived we'd all caroused outside Reg's caravan – just us Brits and Serge – while most of the other French dealers had sensibly turned in at nine, determined to get a good night's sleep.

Serge had been worried about Diddy. He was wondering where he was, though Algie and I had a pretty good idea and kept raising eyebrows, exchanging glances and wry, knowing smiles whenever he mentioned his wayward son.

'Don't worry about him,' I told Serge. 'He's a grown man; he can take care of himself.'

'He's up to no good, I'm sure of it,' he moaned for the umpteenth time. 'He's only twenty-three, he hardly knows he's born.'

Reg asked what he was saying. When Algie translated in a somewhat patronising superior manner, Reg, in a semi-drunken state, insisted on going over and ruffling Serge's hair and giving him the benefit of his advice. 'Ah, let him be, Sergey, if you can't wreak havoc when you're young, you sure as hell won't know how to do it when you get old.' He finished with a maniacal laugh.

I didn't tell Serge we had seen Diddy chatting up the gypsy girls. He was worried enough as it was, and I was certain there was nothing he could do to rein him in.

'What time is it?' Helen was stirring.

'Six,' I said, looking at my watch. 'I'll make a cup of tea.'

I put the kettle on and looked out of the caravan door. In the dim morning light I could see people arriving. The other market tradesmen were getting their stands ready for the onslaught and a few early buyers with torches were examining the displays. I felt a bit knackered after getting to bed so late. I was regretting not having followed the example of the other wiser dealers. Thank God I no longer drank! Real hangovers were a thing of the past. At least I hadn't fallen off the wagon recently.

I passed Helen her tea in bed and staggered out with mine to take the covers off our stand and prepare for the early *chineurs* (bargain hunters). Reg and Algie were either side of us and Serge had parked his van across the way and set up his stand alongside it. He was still asleep. I could hear loud, drawn-out snores from inside. There was no sign of Diddy. He hadn't turned up last night and I hoped for his sake some enraged gypsy father hadn't found him wherever he was. He might return with a stiletto in his neck, or worse. Actually, I couldn't imagine anything worse. I tried not to think about it.

I began opening boxes of delicate china and placing them piece by piece carefully on a table. I'd learnt from a history of expensive breakages to unwrap them with the cardboard box placed on the ground. Things tended to slip through my fumbling fingers, especially in the early morning, and if they were already down on the floor they didn't have far to fall. It didn't always work, but a breakable item dropped from table height invariably smashed into a million pieces.

'Hey, what's happening, man?' I looked up and recognised a French picture dealer, Pierro, who regularly bought from me. He was an amiable character who'd told me he had spent several years in San Francisco during the sixties. He was now over seventy but didn't look it. He spoke English with an exaggerated American accent and said he used to drink beer and play pool all day, but now he had to work hard for a living. He was sometimes accompanied by his girlfriend, an attractive Spanish lawyer who was a good thirty years younger than he was. He was examining an Impressionist oil painting of a river scene with willow trees. Helen had bought it at a house sale and I was quite fond of it myself. We had tried to track down the artist but the signature was indistinct. At least I hadn't faked it, which was what a lot of *brocanteurs* I knew did.

'Hey, I like this,' he said, examining it with his torch. 'How much do you want for it?'

He had told me he sold oil paintings on the Spanish market, mostly in Madrid, and I knew he got ridiculous prices for anything half decent. As I was thinking how much he'd be willing to pay for it my attention was caught by a figure skulking among the pines. Emerging from the shadows it snuck along towards Serge's van. It was Diddy. But this wasn't the Diddy I knew. His normally pristine white tracksuit and trainers looked crumpled, like he'd been dragged through a hedge backwards. He opened the back of Serge's van, climbed in, looked out to see if anyone had seen and pulled the door shut behind him.

'So, how much do you want for it, the painting?'

'Oh, er, sorry...' I was caught on the hop. I quickly pulled a figure out of the air and he immediately took out a wodge of euros and peeled off the amount I'd quoted in high denomination notes.

I felt sick. He hadn't attempted to barter. He clearly believed he could make a killing with the painting in Madrid. He tucked it under his arm and made off with it, smiling to himself.

Helen emerged from the caravan. 'I heard you selling something.' She sounded groggy. She's never that good early in the morning. I told her I'd sold the painting and, sheepishly, for how much. She was suddenly wide awake. 'Oh, goody, that's brilliant, a great start. You'll never guess how much profit we made on that!' She was ecstatic.

Phew! No need to tell her how the dealer hadn't quibbled over the price.

People were starting to arrive in droves and Helen and I had our work cut out to cope with the demand. There was a sea of berets bobbing along as the multitude moved through the forest paths, eager to see the wares on offer. There was a festive atmosphere, as if everyone was out to enjoy themselves. I got the impression that this was primarily a local fair patronised by the Landes people and I doubted the character had changed much in a hundred years. The strong smell of cooking churros filled the air. Churros are Spanish in origin and are made from a sticky flour mix which is forced through a machine to form long fingers of batter, which are then deep fried and sprinkled with sugar or coated in chocolate and eaten from a paper bag. They are a popular if slightly sick-making snack at French fairs. Kiddies love 'em.

As we dealt with the customers I saw Reg had his work cut out as well. I'd noticed him unloading boxes of small collectibles, mixed in with little reproduction items, and miniature brass novelties onto his tables. The punters were thronging round his stand. He caught my eye and gave me the thumbs up. He was taking plenty of the folding stuff.

On the other side Algie wasn't so cheerful. His expensive paintings and bronzes weren't flying out. The crowds drifted straight past without giving his display a second glance. Every time I was wrapping up a sale I noticed him watching me with a miserable expression. There's nothing worse than seeing someone selling their wares like hotcakes when no one's interested in your own stuff. When it happens to me and Helen we ask ourselves what we are doing wrong and what the other dealer is doing right. But there are *brocanteurs* who just get jealous, blaming the successful colleague whom they think is succeeding in taking away their trade. It doesn't make sense, and if you try to explain to them it's just market forces and maybe they haven't got what the customer wants, they get annoyed.

Across the way I could see Serge doing good business, too. There was no sign of Diddy and I assumed he was in the van sleeping off his night of bacchanal and debauchery.

By mid-morning the fair was jammed with people slowly wending their way between the stands. You could barely move in the aisles and it was so packed it was beginning to feel uncomfortable. Across the way I caught a glimpse of Diddy with a sick expression on his face. At least he was up, and Serge had managed to get him working and taking money.

Reg and Rita next door were doing well, but Algie was still standing looking glumly at the crowds passing his stand. If someone stopped, he hovered nearby with an expectant expression on his face. But when they lost interest and moved on he watched them go, annoyed and cursing them under his breath like they were idiots for missing out on a great opportunity to purchase one of his fabulous paintings or bronzes. He caught my eye and shouted out, 'Bloody ignorant peasants! It's like throwing pearls before swine!'

I was trying to focus on packing an Edwardian cut-glass flask for a little old lady. I didn't want to forget to wrap the ground-glass stopper separately and put it in the bag. I nodded, still concentrating, and grinned at Algie in agreement.

It was almost midday and Helen and I were thinking it was bound to ease up a bit soon when we heard angry, raised voices. People were turning, craning round in the direction of Serge's stand.

Reg, Rita and Algie had heard it too and looked across at me. The shouting grew more intense. I caught a glimpse of Diddy arguing with a burly man in a suit.

I turned to Helen. 'Will you be all right for a minute? I'm just going to see what's happening.'

'Be careful, don't get involved,' she warned. 'You know what they're like.'

'I'll be fine,' I insisted as I headed for Serge's stand.

'What's going on?' I asked when I got there. The *gitans* in France don't sport tattoos or body piercings. The older ones are tough and look more like East End London thugs from the fifties. They favour thin moustaches and swept back hairstyles. This man was one of those.

Serge pulled me to one side. 'I don't know, Johnny. I've known this *gitan* for years, he regularly buys violins from me.'

The man looked over at us with a face like thunder. He was cursing under his breath.

'Now he's accusing Diddy of shortchanging him. I came over as Diddy was completing the sale of that violin.' He pointed at the instrument the man was holding like a club ready to hit Diddy. 'He's a good client of mine; it's a problem.'

The *gitan* approached me like I might be able to help. He was incandescent with anger. 'I gave this *résidu de fausse couche* a two-hundred-euro note but he refuses to give me my change.'

'You liar!' Diddy yelled, standing up close, right in the man's face. He didn't like being called a 'leftover from a miscarriage' one little bit. 'You gave me a hundred-euro note and I gave you fifty back.' He was facing up to him ready for a *bagarre* (fight). But judging by his size, my money was on the *gitan* if it came to fisticuffs. He was rough and tough.

It crossed my mind that somewhere along the line they might have fallen foul of a typical shortchange trick and I wasn't sure which one was the trickster. I'd been stitched up by it myself a few times. I had learnt to hold on to a large denomination euro note in full view of the customer when giving change. Once the transaction was over the note could then be put away and there could be no argument. The customer couldn't claim he had given you more money than he had.

'How many two-hundred-euro notes have you got then, Diddy?' I said, attempting to soothe the situation. He pulled out a fistful of euros and waved them with disdain in the man's face. He had clearly had a good morning. The *gitan* went to grab his money, Diddy pushed him, and the man snapped and went to hit him. From behind me Reg appeared in a blur right between the pair of them. He was grinning insanely. With his shaven head he looked unhinged, ready to do some serious damage. One touch could tip him over the edge. It wasn't a pleasant prospect.

The *gitan* looked taken aback, thought better of it, turned on his heel and was off, disappearing into the crowd.

Serge was upset. '*Putain!* That's another good client lost.' He turned to Diddy. 'What's the matter with you, you want to drag the good name of Bastarde right through the mud?' Diddy looked hurt. He sneered and walked off in a huff.

Reg wasn't sure what had happened. His eyes were still glowing from the adrenalin rush as I explained the situation to him.

'Oh dear, looks like I done a bit of boo-boo there.' He put his arm round Serge's shoulders. 'Sorry, mate, I didn't know he was a good customer of yours.'

Serge gave a dry smile. '*Le pirate*, he's always ready for a *bagarre*, eh?' He was flattered, really, that Reg had come to help.

'That's a pity,' said Reg to me. 'Those *gitans* don't like to lose face. That won't be the last we'll be seeing of that bloke.'

I shrugged. It was beyond me. I hadn't a clue. I was just glad the incident hadn't ended in violence.

It was *midi* and the crowds were starting to thin, heading for various buffet and restaurant tents. I made my way back to our caravan where Helen was preparing a meal. When I explained in detail what had happened we were once again amazed at Reg's behaviour. 'He's like a wild animal,' said Helen, 'but you can't help admiring him, and we like wild animals.' She laughed. 'Pity he upset that *gitan*, though. If I was Serge, I'd be worried now.'

Algie came across, grinning in triumph. 'I just sold a very nice bronze to a client with good taste,' he said smugly. 'Better to wait for class than sell cheap tat to the peasants, what.' He was crowing.

It was lunchtime and the atmosphere was laid-back, relaxed. Families with kids in tow were out to enjoy the fun of the fair. People mooched past eating churros or *barbe à papa* (candy floss). Over in a clearing the roundabouts and sideshows were in full swing. Helen and I sat out front watching the passers-by, drinking in the atmosphere. It was great living and working here in France. The weather was brilliant and the people of the Landes were warm and friendly and appeared to respect each other. The French have somehow managed to retain some of the old-world values we Brits have lost. We sometimes tried to fathom what gave them a different approach to life from us Anglo-Saxons. Was it because they had guillotined their aristocracy and destroyed the class system? Or was it the influence of their strong Roman Catholic background? Or was it the weather? We couldn't be sure. But we had been living in France so long now we felt just as at home here as we did in England.

'I like the forest,' I said.

Helen said she did too. 'We haven't looked at houses out here yet. What do you reckon?'

'I thought you didn't like the woods,' I said. 'We ruled this area out before when we looked because of that.'

'Yeah, well I was thinking like a typical Londoner then. I couldn't believe there weren't people lurking in the woods at night. I used to feel like that about open countryside until I discovered it was my imagination playing tricks. Now I think I might have changed my mind about woods, too. There's a sort of special air about them.'

'I know what you mean,' I agreed.

'We'll give it a go then, when the fair's finished?' she said.

'Yes, it won't hurt to look.'

Reg came over and sat with us in the sunshine. 'Done all right, have you?' he asked. He appeared to have put the incident with the *gitan* behind him.

'It's been fun taking all that money and ummm... really interesting,' said Helen.

'It's not over yet, darlin' – there's always a second wave in the afternoon.'

'Really?' said Helen warily. 'I can't believe it, but if you say so...'

Reg swigged at a can of lager. His freshly shaved pale pate had caught the sun and was starting to glow pink. He shouted across to Rita. 'All right, babe? Keep on working, raking in the old lolly!' He laughed when she gave him a V-sign.

Over at Serge's stand Diddy had got over his fit of pique and was chatting up the pair of 'jailbait' girls. He had turned up a ghetto blaster pumping out loud rap and hip hop. He appeared to be trying to drown out the repetitive over-jolly *fête* music being broadcast over the fair's sound system. He was grooving along, showing off his choice moves, impressing the gypsy girls, who watched with rapt attention.

Algie was walking back from lunch and saw them, wolf-whistled and began to gyrate his hips in a suggestive manner like he was down the Flamingo or the Roaring Twenties in Carnaby Street. I looked round to see Helen and Rita gesticulating to each other, sticking their fingers down their throats pretending to vomit. They obviously thought Algie was the pits. He said he had been to one of the restaurant tents where I realised he had been eating alone. He looked sneeringly at the remains of our simple meal.

'Oh, I had champagne and oysters,' he boasted. 'Absolutely delicious!'

'That's all your profit gone down your throat then,' said Helen scathingly.

'Oh my dear, if only I had a lovely little caravan like yours,' he said disparagingly, 'I'd be able to live on bread and cheese like the rest of you paupers.'

I thought Helen might give him a mouthful back, but she fell about laughing. Algie roared with laughter too. They appeared to be warming to each other. She was pleased to have found someone she could give a good bit of South London backchat to.

Algie plonked himself down in a camping chair and belched loudly. He was clearly sated, the worse for wear.

'How many bottles of champagne have you had?' asked Reg. 'You could have brought one back for us, you greedy git.'

'Get your own,' snorted Algie.

Serge came over and we men hung out on Algie's stand waiting for the afternoon rush to pick up, leaving Helen and Rita to cope on their own.

'Your Diddy's got his mind on the job all right,' said Reg to Serge, waving across at the lad, who was still showing off to the gypsy girls. I translated for Serge, leaving out the irony.

He shrugged. 'You're only young once, Johnny... *le pirate* is right. I was just the same when I was Diddy's age. But if he loses me any more regular clients like that *gitan* this morning I'll be going bankrupt.'

People were coming back from their relaxed French lunch hour and the aisles were starting to fill up again. I had noticed Rita and Helen were giving us desperate looks but we carried on chatting away. As we gazed at the crowd we saw the tough *gitan* approach, closely followed by two other men.

'What did I tell you?' said Reg. 'That bloke wasn't going to take that lying down.' He was trying to hold down his excitement at the prospect.

'Maybe we should keep out of it,' I said, thinking that if Reg got involved it was bound to end in violence.

Serge went over to join Diddy.

'Nah, come on, Sergey needs us,' said Reg, already on his way. I had to run to keep up and Algie was following with long strides.

'What's all this excitement about, old chap?' He had sobered up very quickly.

We lined up in front of Serge's stand with Diddy behind us, and Serge joined us. We were like the Musketeers.

The *gitans* stopped dead, eyeing up Reg.

We had an audience. I could see Helen and Rita standing on chairs, trying to see what was happening over the heads of the crowd.

The *gitan* spoke to Serge. 'I've come to apologise. I made a mistake this morning. I found this two-hundred-euro note in my pocket. I knew I only had the one and I could have sworn I used it to pay for the violin. I'm really sorry for all the bother earlier.'

Algie, Serge and I visibly relaxed and Diddy looked triumphant. But Reg was ready, poised to go in for the kill. He hadn't understood a word. The other two young *gitans* looked worriedly at him.

I turned to Reg. 'It's OK, it was all a mistake. He had the two hundred note in his pocket.'

Reg looked at me in disbelief. 'What?'

I repeated what I'd just said, putting my hand on his arm to calm him. He looked deflated. I'd seen this hyped-up state before, mostly in our Staffordshire bull terriers.

Everyone was laughing now and chatting with the *gitans*. The two younger men with Serge's client were his brothers and it had turned all chummy and 'lads together'.

The burly *gitan*'s name was Lorenzo. He introduced us to his younger brothers, Syd and Fabio. They were charming and Lorenzo insisted he treat us to dinner as a way of making up. I had a feeling he didn't want to alienate Serge, who had obviously unknowingly undersold him some valuable violins over the years. I explained that Reg and I had our wives with us and he nodded dismissively at them. 'They can come too.'

Later Fabio came round with a card with an address jotted down on it. They had booked us all into a celebrated local restaurant in the little village of Rion-des-Landes. When Serge saw the name he was impressed.

'It's Chez Maïté, run by a famous French TV chef. The food, *c'est le top*.'

When we'd all finished packing away we turned up at the restaurant and perused the menu outside, waiting for the *gitans* to arrive.

'Blimey,' said Reg, 'I could never afford to eat here.'

A big Mercedes white van pulled up across the road and Lorenzo and his brothers piled out. They came swaggering across, and Lorenzo was greeted as a valued customer by the maître d', who showed us to the best table in the house.

Syd and Fabio had taken to Diddy. The three of them nattered fast together in French so peppered with slang I could barely understand what they were on about. Serge and Lorenzo, meanwhile, talked business, while the English contingent – me, Reg and Algie – sat together with Helen and Rita, who were chatting and laughing, cracking jokes about the men.

Algie began to pontificate about 'young people these days'.

'They don't seem to have any self-discipline,' he insisted, looking across at Diddy. 'When I was a boy we had discipline instilled in us. If I crossed my father, I got a good hiding. We soon learnt to do what we were told.'

'I never had to beat my boy,' said Reg. 'But when he grew up I always told him if he got caught, keep your head down, do your bird and get out. It's the only way.'

'I didn't need to beat my boys,' said Algie. 'I kept them under control with the voice. They didn't dare cross me. It wasn't worth it.'

'My dad used to beat the living daylights out of me and my brother with a heavy leather slipper,' I said. 'He'd storm in and lay into us, knocking ten bells out of us for no apparent reason. He'd throw us across the room into the wall and once he knocked me out.'

I looked up. Reg and Algie were staring at me, shocked.

'What?' I said. 'I thought that was normal.'

'I don't think that's right, mate,' said Reg gently.

Algie looked embarrassed. 'Yes, a bit excessive, old chap.'

'Helen says that too,' I said.

There was an awkward silence between us. I pulled out my trusty ever-ready harmonica and started to play 'Baby Please Don't Go', the old Big Joe Williams number. Within a few minutes everyone in the restaurant was smiling and clapping. The staff were jolly, Lorenzo and his brothers were ecstatic. *Laissez les bontemps rouler!* (Let the good times roll!) Music gave me an escape route and always saved me. It was a universal language and a cure for all ills.

The evening ended full of geniality and bonhomie. We all parted in good spirits, handshaking, kissing and hugging. As we drove home Helen squeezed my leg. 'I'll get on to the estate agents round here first thing tomorrow,' she said. 'It feels like we could have a nice life hidden away here in the woods.'

I agreed with her but inside I felt sad, knowing that soon I was going to have to leave our house in the Chalosse where I was safe and comfortable. It had been the only place – apart from Helen's flat in Clapham and our windmill in Portugal miles from anywhere – that I felt at home.

It all felt a bit daunting and I couldn't say exactly why.

'So can we get another Staffordshire bull terrier as well then?' I asked.

'Ooh, I've wanted one for ages,' said Helen. 'It's been so long without one since Spike. I'd really like that – a new house, and a new dog to love.'

'You're on,' I shouted, punching the air. 'YES! To the woods!'

13

A BIT OF A HANDFUL

This wasn't quite working out the way we had hoped. Our Staffordshire bull terrier puppy was attacking our feet, trying to bite our shoes as we walked. He barked and jumped with glee, tail wagging furiously, clearly excited, as if this was what we wanted. He was a 'red' (tan-coloured) Staff and we had christened him Buster – the way he was turning out we couldn't have chosen a better name. We had bought him from a Staffie breeder at le Petit Crécy in the middle of France.

To be fair, this behaviour wasn't his fault. We'd had to leave him with dog sitters while we returned to England on a buying trip when we'd only had him for two weeks. We needed to spend a few days bidding in the auction rooms in the UK, scouring through the antique fairs and car boots for bargains that might go down well in France. We couldn't take him with us as we had to wait until he was six months old to have his first rabies jab. Then we had to wait a whole year for them to issue him with a special 'doggy passport'.

We found English dog sitters living in the Gers, a couple, Malcolm and Brenda, who had recently bought a small country cottage and moved out to France. Brenda seemed kindly and capable, but we weren't totally sure about Malcolm. He never stopped talking from the moment we arrived. He appeared to have a completely over-romanticised view of France and everything French.

'I love it here,' he insisted. 'The builders are real trained professionals, not cowboys. You wouldn't catch me going back to England... no way!' He admitted he couldn't speak a word of French, but he was determined to learn with the set of CDs he'd just bought.

'I love dogs,' he said, down on his knees play-fighting with Buster. 'I've always had German shepherds – marvellous dogs! So intelligent and easy to train.'

'Best not fight with Staffs,' I advised him gently. 'They get overexcited and don't know when to stop.'

'I could play fight with my Alsatians for hours,' he insisted. 'I only had to give them the command and they stopped immediately.'

'It doesn't work like that with Staffordshire bull terriers,' I said. 'Trust me, we've had eight and it's best not to get them too worked up. When their eyes glaze over they kind of lose it.'

'My dogs were well trained and totally obedient,' he persisted. 'I could do anything with them. Don't worry, when you get back you won't believe the change in this little chap.'

'There's really no need,' we said. 'Just feed him and exercise him, he'll be fine.'

Brenda was more practical. 'The garden's fenced so he can have the run of the place. He won't be any trouble.'

As we drove off with them waving at the garden gate holding up Buster and waggling his little paw goodbye Helen had second thoughts. 'I'm not happy,' she said. 'Let's cancel the trip and take Buster home.'

'He'll be all right,' I said. 'They're dog lovers. What harm can it do?'

We returned a week later with a van full of English goodies and were keen to see how Buster had got on. Helen had been phoning regularly while we were away to be reassured by Brenda that he was 'going great guns'. And it was true, he looked fit and healthy and even appeared to have grown. He was jumping up at the gate watched over by Malcolm, who was smiling proudly. As we walked up the garden path Buster attacked our feet, leaping back, growling and barking, going in for the kill, nipping at our toes right through our shoes.

'He's a right little devil, isn't he?' said Malcolm. In through the back door he pointed at a pile of assorted trainers strewn across the floor.

'I haven't got a decent pair left; he loves to have a good old set-to with my shoes.' He held up his foot in a torn tennis shoe and kicked out at Buster, who responded with a chorus of furious growls, biting the rubber sole and tugging at it. Malcolm then went in to play-attack him, slapping him round the head, pinching his hindquarters, knocking his feet from under him. Buster reacted like a maniac, biting Malcolm's sleeve and pulling it violently with all his strength and letting out menacing deep-throated growls.

Helen gave me a wide-eyed look. What had we done, leaving our puppy with someone who hadn't grasped what a Staff was all about? Buster was hyped up and out of control. When I tried to call him he ignored me and threw me evil little backward glances as if to say, 'Who the hell are you... do I know you?'

When I clipped his lead on his collar he reacted badly, twisting and turning, biting with eyes bulging like he thought I was carting him off to his doom.

'He doesn't like the lead, does he?' said Malcolm, chuckling.

Well, he was walking with a lead and collar before we left, even though he was so young, I thought to myself. In one week Malcolm appeared to have undone our puppy's basic training. We managed to carry him out to the van and set off for home. Buster sat up front panting, staring out at the scenery flashing by.

'I can't believe it,' said Helen. 'How has this happened? He was all sweet and cuddly when we left him.'

Buster began to drool. 'Poor little chap, he's overexcited and he's not used to looking out of a moving vehicle,' said Helen. Suddenly he gave a strange moan and vomited all over the dashboard. We jumped to avoid the splashback. (This wasn't a new phenomenon for us. One of our Staffs, Iggy, had suffered with car sickness, but he loved travelling and you couldn't keep him out of the car.) We pulled up and attempted to mop up the mess, but it was a hot day and as we drove on the smell was overpowering. Buster was tired now and had settled down across Helen's lap.

'I hope we can get his confidence back again,' I said.

'He doesn't know who he belongs to,' said Helen. 'It's just like when children are moved from pillar to post and don't know who cares for them. He's like a problem child, an emotional mess.'

'He'll be all right,' I said. 'He'll soon settle down.' I was trying to sound confident but I wasn't so sure. The next day he wasn't any better. If you tried to walk anywhere, he sprang along backwards ahead of you barking and biting your feet, mostly in play, but often his sharp little teeth actually snapped shut on your foot causing considerable pain. We tried talking to him gently, soothing and calming him, begging him to desist. I even resorted to shouting, but it made things worse. He thought it was all part of the game of rough house.

We were at our wits' end. 'This is the last Staff puppy I'll ever have,' I announced, rubbing my sore toes. Helen found a possible solution for a misbehaving dog. 'You get a water pistol and squirt him with it whenever he's naughty and say "No!" firmly. They reckon it's a painless way to discipline a dog.' We bought one and tried it. As soon as Buster attacked our feet we gave him a squirt and said 'No!' firmly. He ignored us. In fact, he thought we were playing and ran round in circles, barking furiously. We believe it was this that started his obsession with hoses. Whenever we use one in the garden he attacks the spray as if it were alive, biting the nozzle until he rips the end off.

This wasn't his only obsession. Sniffing around our field he discovered holes in the ground, the homes of ground squirrels or *lérots*, small rodents that look a bit like meerkats. They are strictly nocturnal and we have never seen one, they hide so well, although we once found the corpse of one the cats had killed. Buster was excited by their scent and liked to set about digging dementedly in an attempt to unearth them. However many times we caught him and ordered him to stop it made no difference; he would come inside all covered in dirt and mud, excited and panting as if we should be impressed. Then I'd forget, and walking across the field I'd step in one of the Buster-enlarged burrows and nearly break my leg. Once I heard a scream and ran out to find Helen had tripped in one of these holes and badly twisted her ankle. We took to shutting Buster in the house to keep him out of mischief, but his surplus energy built up until he began frantically twisting round in circles trying to bite his own tail.

Gradually, with love and kindness, he started to trust us a bit more and by walking him down the lanes behind our house and getting him to 'heel' on the lead we began to calm him down. He even stopped throwing those evil little backward glances. The lanes ran through deciduous woods filled with oaks and horse chestnuts, a favourite spot for local hunters. We were taking him for his evening walk when a figure appeared on the brow of the hill.

'It's that horrible farmer bloke from the next village,' cried Helen.

'Oh no!' My heart sank.

'And he's got his dog with him.'

I grabbed Buster and snapped the lead onto his collar. The man was an oafish, taciturn character who always had an evil-looking rifle over his shoulder on the lookout for pheasant or deer, regardless if it was the hunting season or not. His dog was a giant mastiff-cross, a brute of a beast. I pulled Buster's lead tight and called him to heel. I was worried because the farmer's dog, a dominant male, believed that this was his territory. Buster was a puppy and if it came to a fight he wouldn't stand a chance. We froze as the dog spied us from afar and came bounding down the hill to investigate. Buster saw him coming and dropped down, crouching. The dog ran up to him, barking loudly. He was sizing Buster up, scolding him before he taught him a big lesson. I prayed his owner would call him to order and save us, but he was strolling down the hill with a big stupid grin on his face, enjoying our discomfort. The big dog loomed over Buster, who lay there silent, just waiting. As he came in to attack, Buster sprang to life, launching himself at the dog's throat. I tugged hard on the lead and stopped him as his jaws snapped shut a hair's breadth from the dog's jugular. The brute jumped back in surprise, let out a loud squeal, and ran away with his tail between his legs, cowed. The farmer stopped dead in his tracks, his mouth open. Our little puppy had seen his monster dog off. I couldn't believe it either, but I was secretly proud at this turn of events, even though I didn't really want Buster to learn to fight. He was a true Staff!

I grinned at the farmer. 'It's OK, don't worry, he's had his dinner.'

He looked flummoxed. He wasn't sure if I was joking or not. He sneered, turned on his heel and strode off back up the hill closely followed by his dog, which had decided to pretend the incident never happened.

'Did you have to say that?' said Helen.

'Well, he has had his dinner.'

'Yes, a good joke, but no need to antagonise him. Did you see him hefting his rifle? If there had been a fight, I think he might have used it.'

'Oh, come on!' I said. But the thought made me go hot and cold.

14

MAYHEM IN THE MARKETS

We walked Buster every day, continuing to train him to heel and getting him used to being controlled on the lead again. Staffs react well to discipline as long as it's administered with love and understanding. He took to carrying a walking stick in his mouth. This was his special task and he was obsessed yet again. If I tried to take it from him, he hung on for grim death. At least he was barking and biting our shoes a bit less. We had managed to undo some of the bad habits he had learnt from Malcolm. He was still a rugged little terrier but no longer *têtu* (headstrong), as the French say.

The following Thursday was the day of the monthly Dax market and I suggested to Helen I take Buster with me in the van to get him used to being out and about and meeting new people. I was confident he wouldn't be any trouble. He had got over his initial car sickness and now loved to sit up on the front seat next to me.

'Just keep an eye on him and don't let him out to run around,' said Helen. 'He still gets overexcited.'

This was true. Although he wasn't very good with other dogs, he loved people. All our previous Staffs had been the same. They are one of the friendliest breeds and like nothing better than making new chums.

Dawn was breaking as I drove into the town centre. As usual, Buster had his head stuck out the window, taking in the sights. He was on the lookout for other dogs. Whenever we passed one his head swivelled and I could almost see the cartoon dotted line from his bulging eyes staring straight at every unsuspecting animal.

I parked my van in my usual place opposite my pitch and began unloading my tables and boxes of stock. Monsieur Repro next door was already halfway through setting up his cunning mix of real antiques and *pompes* (fakes). He was serious about relieving the customers of as much money, and as early in the day, as possible. His real name was Laurent, and he wasn't setting up his stand himself; his young assistant from Toulouse was doing all the work while he just watched, relaxing in one of his reproduction antique armchairs. Now and again he got up, irritated, and showed his poor assistant how he wasn't doing something properly, pushing him to one side. I don't know how he did it but he was the only *brocanteur* with a connection to the electrical supply linked to the overhead lights and his assistant was arranging a series of tiny twinkling spotlights which bathed his wares in a soft, warm glow. The result was that his stand looked professional and highly seductive. He regularly got ridiculous money for his fakes, which he always insisted were genuine to any prospective customer. He loved to boast about his triumphs to other dealers in the tapas bar at lunchtime. He was generally disliked, but I thought secretly some of the *brocanteurs* admired his success and were even tempted to emulate him. Serge himself spoke about Laurent with admiration and the pair of them sometimes spent the night up at the Dax casino after a good day's sales, gambling away all their profits.

I was wondering where Serge was when I saw his beaten-up old Renault van with SERGE BASTARDE – BROCANTEUR in big letters on the side circling the square. It turned at the traffic lights, drove along the service road that ran round the market and parked behind my van. Serge climbed out and shouted across to me. He was wearing his *béret extra large*, the one he bought at the Lourdes sale, an old pair of jeans and a striped T-shirt. He looked as stereotypically French as Lord Snooty always looked stereotypically English. All he was missing was the string of onions round his neck. I could see Diddy in the passenger seat, his head nodding on his chest, half asleep.

'Eh Johnny!' Serge waved as he opened up the back of his van and began unloading his boxes of bric-a-brac. He ran round, opened the passenger door and shook Diddy, who reluctantly climbed out and began helping him. As Diddy passed my van window he did a double-take when he saw Buster sitting up front in the driver's seat. He tapped on the window and Buster gazed at him, unmoved. It didn't look like he was ever going to be a good guard dog. Diddy's face broke out in a big grin. When he turned I saw he was wearing a hooded *'pull'*, as the French call them, with the silhouette of a pit bull on the front. He came across smiling. 'He your pit bull, man? Nice dog.'

'He's not a pit bull,' I said, 'he's a Staff.'

'Oh right, an American Staff, nice dog.'

'No, he's a Staffy Anglais,' I corrected him. 'They're almost the same, just a bit smaller.'

Serge came over, excited. 'My God, Johnny, is he yours this pit bull dog?'

'He's not a pit bull,' I repeated for his benefit.

'Has he passed his driving test?' Diddy asked with a grin.

'He's a Staffy Anglais,' I explained again. 'Come on over and say hello, he likes people.'

'I'm not sure, Johnny,' said Serge. 'Does he bite?'

'Of course he doesn't, he's a sweetheart.'

I opened the van door and wound down the window. Buster stuck his head out, wanting a fuss. Diddy and Serge leant back warily.

'Come on, he won't hurt you,' I said. 'He just wants a stroke.'

Diddy, full of bravado, managed to overcome his fear and scratched Buster behind the ears.

This was just a short step away from Buster trying to climb onto his shoulder and lick him to death. They took to each other. Serge insisted on getting him out of the van and

Buster was all over them, jumping up, snorting with delight. He had decided the pair would make ideal playmates and when they began mock-fighting with him he was overjoyed. We had just spent weeks training some sense into him and now Serge and Diddy were undoing all our good work.

'Best not fight with him,' I said. But they weren't listening. Serge was rolling on the floor kicking out and laughing as Buster worried at his trainers while Diddy was slapping at him, holding onto his collar and pulling him away. Serge's *béret extra large* fell off and Buster snatched it up and began a tug of war, growling and shaking his head from side to side, trying to break Serge's grip. He was overexcited and I had a feeling it was going to end in tears.

'Perhaps you should let him calm down for a bit,' I said, grabbing his collar. Buster's eyes had gone wild. It was a state that Staff owners are familiar with, when their dog passes the point of sanity and good sense. It's best to give them a break to pull them back from the brink. I dragged Buster away and put him back in the van. He was straight up at the window looking at them, wild-eyed.

'Oh, he's adorable!' said Serge.

'Yeah, cool dog,' said Diddy. He went across and fussed Buster, who stuck his head out and licked his face.

'Can we take him over and show Thibaud?' asked Diddy. 'I'll pretend he's mine.'

'I'd rather you didn't,' I said. I was remembering what Helen had said about not letting him run around.

'Oh, go on, Johnny,' said Serge, 'we'll look after him.' He was excited, like a big schoolboy. It was nice to see him like that. What harm could it do?

'All right, keep him on the lead and don't let him run around.'

'Don't worry, we won't, you can trust us,' said Diddy.

I watched the pair of them set off across the market with Buster, head down, pulling out front. Could they control him? What was I thinking of? Of course they couldn't! I rushed across the square. When I caught up with them Diddy and Thibaud were holding the ends of an antique walking stick with Buster gripping the middle, hanging on with his teeth. His feet were off the ground, but he wouldn't let go, shaking his head so his whole body twisted and jerked like a crazy puppet. My friend Louis the bookseller turned round, laughing. 'Have you seen this pit bull, John? He's a maniac!'

'Yoiks! Tally-ho!' Lord Snooty was striding across the market square. 'I say, a Staffordshire bull terrier, isn't it? Now that's what I call a real English dog... indomitable, with a great heart. Much better than those pathetic little French bulldog things.'

'I rather like *le bouledogue français*,' I said.

'No, they're pitiful creatures. The French prefer poodles. This Staffy can't be Serge's, he must be yours, John.'

'OK. Yes, he's mine. His name's Buster,' I said.

'Oh, what an awful, common name! Couldn't you have thought up something a bit classier?'

'I would have thought a Labrador was more your sort of thing,' I said.

'You're forgetting I'm a Londoner. Ask Helen, we've always loved Staffordshire bull terriers in London.' He went over and grabbed one end of the stick with Serge. 'C'mon Buster m'lad, let's see what you're made of.' He began to shake the stick violently. I pulled at Buster's collar but he still wouldn't let go.

'He's a spunky little chap, isn't he?' said Snooty.

A small crowd of *brocanteurs* had gathered round to watch the spectacle, joking amongst themselves.

'Oi, oi! No dog fighting allowed!' It was Reg. He ran in and grabbed the other end of the stick with Serge. Buster was hanging on for grim death and kicking both back legs, desperate to shake them off. There was a loud crack, the stick broke and Buster dropped to the floor and gleefully ran off with one end, his lead dragging behind him. Lord Snooty, Serge, Diddy, Thibaut, Reg and me chased after him, but he dodged us all easily; to him it was a great game. He ran between the tables, waving the end of the stick and daring us to catch him. My heart sank. The road was ahead and it was now eight in the morning and busy with rush-hour traffic. I shouted for Buster to stop. He paused for a split second and looked back. Then he was off again, veering towards Monsieur Repro's beautifully arranged stand.

Monsieur Repro didn't see him coming. He was sitting back in his chair with his feet up on a gout stool, looking the other way. Buster's paws caught one of the electrical leads and a series of spotlights zipped up in the air one after another, crashing down and popping out. Monsieur Repro was up on his feet, mouth wide open, hands above his head. '*Qu'est-ce que c'est? Qu'est-ce que c'est?*'(What is it?) He was apoplectic. A large, expensive-looking vase was swaying precariously. It overbalanced, fell and was caught by Monsieur Repro's assistant in the nick of time. A stack of shelves displaying bronze and spelter figures began to rock alarmingly before Monsieur Repro leapt forward and managed to steady them. An expensive looking gilt French ormolu clock decorated with winged cherubs toppled and would have fallen if Reg hadn't caught it. Thibaut managed to grab Buster's collar and hold him while I clipped his lead on. But he lurched forward and caught the leg of a big cheval mirror in the middle which tipped forward and fell as if in slow motion, hitting the ground and shattering with a loud crash.

'My mirror, my beautiful mirror!' moaned Monsieur Repro. 'Is he yours, this pit bull?' His face was bright red.

'He's not a pit bull,' I said.

'He should be put down!' he screamed. 'He's a menace!'

'Sorry about your mirror,' I said. 'I'll pay for any damage.'

'It was worth a fortune,' insisted Monsieur Repro.

'What, that tat?' chipped in Snooty. 'Don't make me laugh. What utter rubbish! I've been to the same cut-price warehouse where you got it. That's a cheap *pompe.*'

'Let me know how much I owe you Laurent,' I said, leading Buster off.

'Don't worry, old chap,' said Lord Snooty, following me. 'You could smash all his tat and get change out of twenty euros.'

'Maybe, but it's still really embarrassing,' I said. I was just so relieved that Buster hadn't run out into the road. I opened my van and Buster hopped up on the front seat. His eyes were wild and his tongue was hanging out. He'd really enjoyed all the fun. Serge went over and stroked him, getting his face licked clean for his trouble. He turned round, wiping his face with the back of his hand, and there were tears in his eyes. 'Oh, Johnny! Your Buster has brought all the memories flooding back. I miss my Robespierre so much I can't tell you. My heart is breaking – I can't bear life without a dog. I'm never going to see my Robespierre or my little Adrien again.'

He looked so pathetic I put my arm round him. 'You will,' I said, trying to comfort him. 'You will, give it time.'

Later that evening when Helen and I took Buster for a walk he had completely forgotten everything we had taught him. He was back to attacking our feet, barking and acting up.

'What on earth's wrong with him?' asked Helen. 'He's gone backwards. He's out of control again. Did something happen at the market today?'

'I was going to tell you,' I said, caught out. 'He escaped and ran into Mr Repro's stand.' I reluctantly described the whole sorry saga.

'What? I can't believe you let him loose round the market. Look at him, he's all hyped up.'

'I'm expecting to get a bill for the breakages,' I said. 'It was Serge and Diddy's fault. I tried to stop them but they got carried away.'

'Serge and Diddy? What were you thinking of?'

'They both loved Buster and he loved them. But then they play fought with him.'

Helen stopped in her tracks. 'Play fought? Why didn't you stop them? You know what he's like.'

'I know, but Serge really loved Buster. And then he got upset about not having a dog any more, it was really sad.' I bent down to pick up Buster's stick. He saw me reaching for it and as I grabbed it his teeth snapped shut and he wrenched it from my grasp. He ran off, shaking it violently.

'Was Serge really upset?' asked Helen. I could see she had softened.

'Yes, he was in tears.'

'Poor devil. He's not heard anything from Angelique? Surely she'll get in touch. It's not like her.'

'I didn't like to ask him. He was upset enough as it was.'

'There's something not quite right about all this,' said Helen. 'I'll get to the bottom of it eventually.'

I called to Buster and he unexpectedly dropped the stick and came running back. Maybe the setback was only a temporary one. A bit of sensible training and he'd be the model of good behaviour. That's what I was hoping, anyway. I had conveniently omitted to tell Helen how he had nearly run into the road. I didn't want her to think me completely irresponsible.

'Look at him,' I said. He was standing at our feet, looking up at us so sweetly.

'Oh all right, he's a real nightmare but I just can't help it – I love him so much,' said Helen, bending down to fuss him.

15

TEA IN BIARRITZ

Helen and I love Biarritz. It's a wonderful seaside town with its sandy coves, impressive beaches, small harbour and breathtaking views of the Atlantic Ocean across the Bay of Biscay. It's like an exotic Eastbourne inhabited by the rich, the chic and the well-to-do elderly. During July and August the beaches heave with holidaymakers bronzing themselves and cavorting in the foaming surf. But we much prefer Biarritz out of season when the town returns to its normal sleepy state.

We decided to treat ourselves to a day out with Buster as it's just a short drive down the motorway past Bayonne. We spent the morning mooching around the harbour, but when we walked along the promenade Buster went wild, pulling on his lead desperately trying to get to the sea. We wanted to let him run free – dogs are allowed to on the wild sandy beaches that run right up the coast towards Bordeaux, but here there were notices warning that dogs are forbidden on the beach. Buster, who can't read, pulled so hard it made my arms ache and we decided to give up and make our way back up the zigzag communal garden path to the town for some light refreshment. We had parked our car up a shady backstreet and we left Buster with some water, put the sunblinds up on the windows and headed for our favourite place in Biarritz, the Miremont Salon de Thé.

When I was touring the UK with the doo-wop group Darts in the seventies Helen and I loved to frequent the old English tea rooms in the seaside towns. The Miremont is the French equivalent, a wonderful establishment that has been serving the Biarritz gentry for well over a hundred years. We pushed through the glass doors and stopped for a moment to gaze at the incredible display of savoury delicacies and exotic sweet pastries. Then we went upstairs to the restaurant where the decor is belle époque: chandeliers, pink walls and cream-painted wooden panels with Louis XV revival furniture upholstered in pink stripes. It's like stepping back in time to an infinitely more stylish era. The period from the end of the nineteenth century to the beginning of World War One is called *la belle époque* by the French because in retrospect they realised it had been a golden age.

We waited at the top of the stairs to be seated by the maître d'. We were hoping for a table by the picture window with a sea view, but although the restaurant wasn't that busy they were all taken. The maître d' showed us to a table in a corner and we were about to sit down when a high voice called out from across the room.

'*Coucou! C'est moi Johnny!*'

We turned, looking across to a window table where a woman was standing up waving at us. Helen threw me a querying look and I felt myself redden. It was Claudette, Serge's neighbour, in all her glory. I'd recognise her anywhere, even though I'd only met her the once – the night Serge destroyed the beautiful walnut buffet.

'Who on earth's that?' Helen asked quietly.

I gave an embarrassed grin as I realised I hadn't told her about Claudette. The maître d' raised a finger in acknowledgement, swerved off and guided us over to Claudette's table. Then he discreetly withdrew.

I stood self-consciously smiling at Claudette. Up close she was vivid, larger than life, resplendent in a glittering sixties mini-dress and thigh-high boots with a feather boa slung round her neck. She was wearing a turban, bright blue eyeshadow, false eyelashes and pink Day-Glo lipstick.

She grabbed me, pulling me close, kissing me warmly on both cheeks. Her perfume was overpowering. There was a hush in the restaurant. Everyone was staring at us as she leant round me, looking Helen up and down.

'Is this your wife or your mistress, Johnny?' she asked in a loud voice.

'Both!' replied Helen, quick as a flash.

Claudette clapped her hands and laughed, delighted.

'*Formidable!*'

People were smiling now.

'Sit down my dears, you must join me for tea.'

'This is Claudette, Serge's neighbour,' I said, making the introduction. The maître d' swiftly reappeared and slid the chairs into place as Helen and I sat down.

Claudette ordered another pot of tea. 'What about cakes?' she asked. 'No scones though I'm afraid, Johnny. Let's have *gâteau Basque*.' She took charge and ordered.

I pulled a tight smile at Helen.

'You haven't been to visit me yet, Johnny.' She gazed into my eyes and fluttered her false eyelashes. Helen poked me in the leg, raising her eyebrows at me.

'No, well I meant to,' I spluttered.

'Shame on you, Johnny, hiding your charming wife away from me.'

I breathed a sigh of relief.

'I like English people very much,' she said, smiling at us both. 'I love your sangfroid – very different from us French... we get excited so easily.' She opened her eyes wide as if acting in a silent movie. 'I lived in England for many years, you know.'

'Really?' said Helen. 'Whereabouts?'

'I was in London in the sixties.'

'I'm from London,' said Helen. 'What part?'

'Chelsea. I had a little apartment off the King's Road.

'That must have been exciting,' said Helen.

'Gosh, it's really expensive there now,' I said, trying to change the subject.

'Oh yes, it was even then. I had a special friend who looked after me.'

Helen looked askance. She had no idea yet she was talking to a 'lady of the night'.

'Ah yes! The swinging sixties, I remember it well,' I gushed.

'Mmmmm,' agreed Claudette. 'I had some very influential friends. Most of them are gone now.' She pouted sadly.

Helen looked at me, her eyes wide. She was wearing a fixed grin.

'I knew lots of famous people. We were always partying,' said Claudette. 'Dinner dances at the embassies. Men really knew how to treat a lady in those days.' She leant across to Helen and said in a stage whisper, 'Always make them pay my dear, it's only right.'

Helen nodded and glanced at me. 'I certainly will!' She was trying not to laugh – she'd fallen in.

'Oh yes, stars, politicians – I knew them all.'

'Really, like who?' asked Helen. She was genuinely interested now.

'Oh no dear, I couldn't possibly say, we ladies have to be discreet.' She waggled her finger knowingly.

'It must be lovely to live here near the sea like this,' I said gaily. 'Do you come here often?' Helen gave my leg an extra big squeeze and I realised she didn't want me to say 'only in the mating season', one of my favourite Spike Milligan quotes.

'Oh yes, they all know me here. I'm very fond of the maître d'.'

I choked on my tea and Helen had to hit me on the back.

'But it's the young men I love the best,' said Claudette light heartedly.

'Oh yes, don't we all,' said Helen. They both laughed loudly together at this.

'Especially that Diddy, Serge's son. *Il est beau!*' she said with feeling. The three of us laughed at this.

'I'm afraid I have a rendezvous I can't miss,' said Claudette looking at her watch. 'I'm going to have to love you and leave you.'

'We've got to go too,' said Helen.

'I must just visit the little girls' room first,' purred Claudette.

As soon as she'd gone Helen turned to me. 'You never told me about her! I wonder why,' she teased. 'Is there anything you'd like to tell me?'

'No, nothing, I only met her the one time, honest.'

'Oh yes, a likely story.' She was pulling my leg.

'Amazing, she's always trying to drum up custom,' I said.

'Yes, she's wonderful,' said Helen. 'I love her. What a character!'

Claudette reappeared. She was twinkling with freshly applied make-up.

'You don't have to leave just because I am,' she said.

'No really, we have to go as well,' said Helen. 'We've left Buster in the car, he'll be wondering where we are.'

'Buster?' said Claudette, interested. 'Who's Buster, your son?'

'Oh no, I'm afraid not.'

'Buster's our dog,' said Helen.

'Oh, how sweet. I love dogs! My dear little Koko passed on last year. I still miss him most dreadfully.' She threw me a lovelorn look.

She blew a kiss at the maître d' as we got up to leave, but when we stopped to pay he shook his head. '*Non, non, c'est pas nécessaire.*'

Claudette was looking at a display of hand-made chocolates in the foyer. As she went to go through the door a young man in his early twenties bumped into her and she nearly toppled over. But he caught her by the arm and held her upright.

'*Excusez-moi madame*, I'm so sorry, please forgive me.'

Claudette pulled herself together quickly. 'I'm fine, *mon amour.*' She fluttered her eyelashes at him. She half turned to Helen and smiled. 'You see my dear, men are like buses... you wait hours and then they all come at once.' We all laughed again.

As we stood outside on the pavement Claudette clung tightly, kissing me. 'Come up and see me sometime, Johnny,' she cajoled.

'I will, I will,' I said, looking across at Helen.

'You must both come,' said Claudette, turning and embracing Helen. 'I have so enjoyed your company.'

We promised we would.

As we watched her go, tottering up the street in her thigh-high boots, people were waving and calling out greetings to her. She was clearly a well-known and much-loved local character.

'God, she's absolutely brilliant!' said Helen.

'But isn't she a bit sad too?' I asked.

'You think so? I didn't get that. Why do you say that?'

'I don't know,' I said, 'just a feeling. I'm not sure what it is really.'

'I hope we can see her again,' said Helen. 'She invited us both to visit her.'

'Yeah, let's do it... soon,' I said.

16

HANDBAGS AND GLAD RAGS

A couple of weeks later, Serge rang. 'How's Buster?' he asked straight away.

'He's good,' I said. 'He's here with me now.'

'Give him a big pat for me, will you?'

'Of course, Serge, I'm doing it now,' I said, and Buster snorted like a happy little pig.

'Listen, Johnny, you remember my neighbour Claudette? You met her once here with Diddy.'

'How could I forget Claudette?' I said. 'Helen and I bumped into her in the Miremont in Biarritz not long ago. She and Helen really hit it off.'

'It's not good news,' said Serge. 'She's dead.'

'What? No!' I was shocked. 'What happened? She was fine when we saw her.'

'She got the *grippe* – it's going about – and she died. It was very quick. She was eighty-five years old. I suppose she just couldn't fight the virus.'

I didn't know what to say. I couldn't believe it.

'Johnny,' said Serge, 'are you still there?'

'Yes, I'm still here, Serge.' I was thinking about Claudette. I could picture her happily waving goodbye to us in Biarritz. 'That's awful,' I said. 'She was such a great character. We both really liked her.'

'Yes, she certainly was a character,' said Serge. 'I'm going to miss her too.' He paused. 'Look, I was going to ask you a favour, Johnny. Claudette made me promise that when she died I'd go and sort out her stuff before the state got hold of it all. But I'm a bit upset and I can't face it on my own. Diddy's disappeared and I've no idea where he is. Could you come round and help me? I'd feel much happier if you were there.'

'Certainly I will,' I said, without a second thought. Clearing out someone's belongings is never much fun but when you knew and were fond of them... well, that's really tough. 'When are you going to do it?' I asked.

'Would now be too short notice?' he asked.

'All right, Serge,' I said. Helen was checking out houses in the forest. 'Give me an hour, I'll be right over.'

I rang Helen on the mobile and broke the news. She was shaken and agreed I should go straight away. So I locked up and set off in the van with Buster sitting beside me.

The smell of stale perfume was overpowering. It permeated the room and wafted up from the soft furnishings and plush cushions. Serge threw back the heavy curtains and the sun streamed in like the early morning rays of light that chase away the evil darkness of a vampire's tomb. The apartment was vintage opulence from the sixties and seventies.

'She lived here all alone,' said Serge. 'She was always busy entertaining clients, but when they left she was just lonely. Remember that time you met her when she and Diddy came in after a night on the tiles?'

'Yes, that night you destroyed that beautiful walnut buffet,' I said.

'Don't remind me of that, Johnny. Poor Claudette, she never lost her zest for life. She was real class, she was.'

I wasn't sure if 'class' was quite the best word to describe Claudette, but she was certainly special. I had been looking forward to going round to see her with Helen again. Now it was too late.

I followed Serge through to the bedroom, which was dominated by a giant bed covered in black satin. The walls were hung with luscious pink drapes and strewn all over the bed and floor were exotic sequinned cushions. I had the distinct feeling that Claudette had just gone out for a minute and that we were intruding on her private domain.

'She didn't have any relatives,' said Serge. 'I kept her spare key and an eye on the place whenever she was out at one of her do's. She had some very rich clients, men who kept up with her right to the very end.' He pulled a cord and the bedroom curtains swished back. 'She took to Diddy, the two of them got on really well. She had a soft spot for him.'

He opened the drawer on a *chevet* next to the bed. 'She had no gold coins hidden away,' he said, ruefully. 'It was the first thing I checked. She always said that if anything happened to her I was to get in quick and clear her belongings out before the state got hold of them. She said I was to use the money to enjoy myself.'

Yes, that's what she was like, I thought to myself. She had been so full of life. I only hoped I could be half as lively if I reached her age.

There was a huge bird's-eye maple art deco armoire. Serge opened one of the mirrored doors. It was stuffed with what looked like expensive designer dresses. He pulled some out and threw them across the bed. 'Look at these labels... Biba, Mary Quant... She lived in London when she was younger. Nothing but the best for Claudette. She was – how do you say – a dolly bird.'

'Wasn't she a bit too old for that?' I asked.

'Maybe, but she was very well connected. She rubbed shoulders with politicians, show business people, royalty even. She was quite a woman. I enjoyed hearing her exploits over a coffee together. I'll miss her.'

'She must have been more of the Christine Keeler persuasion,' I said.

'Who's that?' said Serge, mystified.

'It's a long story, I'll tell you another time.'

There was a series of mirrored doors along one wall. Serge slid one back and a light came on to reveal shelf upon shelf of pairs of shoes carefully placed alongside one another, some still in their boxes with the lids open and sheets of coloured tissue peeled back. He lifted a pair out and examined them. 'These have never been worn.' He pulled out another pair. 'Or these.' He was amazed. 'Imelda Marcos, eat your heart out!'

Inside the next cupboard were shelves full of stylish leather bags, all painstakingly labelled with stickers with copperplate writing and carefully arranged in neat rows. 'She certainly had a good choice of accessories,' exclaimed Serge. 'There must be hundreds of handbags here.' He examined one. 'This is crocodile skin, very chic.' He snapped open the clip. 'Beautifully crafted. Look at this.' There was a handwritten note tucked inside. 'M. Jean-Marc. Whoa! It says what he liked done to him. He must have given it to her as a gift.' He picked another bag and took out a slip of paper. 'It says Alexis on this. Look at this, she's written his name and his sexual proclivities.' He put his hand in front of his mouth and chuckled. '*Mon dieu!* He had some nasty preferences. What a beast! And look at this one... it says Doudou on this. She must have liked him; she's put three kisses under his name. You know what? There are names in all of these and their sexual tastes. What a professional! She was making sure she used the bag each client had bought her whenever she went out with them and gave them what they liked best. She didn't want to make a mistake and offend them. *Formidable!*'

He pulled out a very classy Hermès bag. 'Wonder who gave her this... *Putain!* I know him – he used to be the mayor in the next village. He's a grandfather with a grown-up family.' He took out another, eager to look inside, and extracted the handwritten note. '*Mon dieu!* I recognise this name too. He was the chief of police. She certainly had some top-drawer clients. This is an eye-opener!' He picked up another bag, zipped open a pocket and withdrew a slip of paper. His eyes widened and he passed me the note. The name Bruno the Basque was written on it in neat handwriting.

'It's Bruno!' yelled Serge excitedly. 'He must have been a regular customer too. See what he likes? If only I could broadcast that around, he'd be a laughing stock.'

I couldn't say I was shocked. The first time I met Bruno he had struck me as a creepy lurker when he boasted about the 'little mini-skirted whore' who had pleasured him in the old quarter of Bayonne. It was no surprise to me that he sought the regular services of a prostitute of Claudette's experience and expertise. But I was surprised he appeared to have given her a handbag as a present. He struck me as the sort of oaf who would never give a woman a thing. Claudette must have been very persuasive for her favours.

'It's this sort of information that can sometimes come in very handy,' said Serge. 'You never know, I might be able to use it one day. Anything to get one over on that *connard*!'

Back in the living room Serge went across to a beautiful highly polished English mahogany roll-top desk. He tried to slide it open but it was locked.

'This is a smart desk, isn't it?'

'It's English, late Victorian, I think. Claudette said she liked English furniture.'

'But where's the key?' asked Serge. He pulled at the drawers but they wouldn't budge.

'Some of these desks are locked from the front,' I explained. 'There's a mechanism which drops down and blocks the drawers as well as the roll-top.'

'*Ah, ouai?*' said Serge. He wasn't listening. He was rummaging through an ashtray full of various bits and pieces... paper clips, odds and ends.

'I've taken them to pieces in the past,' I went on.

'Good, that's interesting.' He had found some keys and went to try them out. He rattled the lock desperately but none of them opened it.

'It must be around somewhere,' I said. 'They have very odd-shaped keys.'

I again had the feeling that I was intruding and that Claudette might walk in any second.

Serge had given up and was rifling through a pile of magazines on a bookshelf. Something prompted me to feel along the underside of the desk top. It was smooth. There was nothing there. I moved along the other side, towards the wall... and my fingers came into contact with a small metal box. It was screwed to the underside of the rim. I dropped down to my knees and examined it. There was a small indentation in the lid, and by inserting a fingernail in it and pulling I was able to slide it open. There was the distinctive brass key inside, which I triumphantly held up to Serge.

'Incredible, Johnny!' He was amazed. 'How did you know about that?'

'I didn't,' I said. 'Maybe Claudette helped me.' Serge had already opened the desk and was sliding the roll-top back to examine its contents. There were lots of pigeonholes and above these several small drawers with ivory knobs. He was rummaging through the papers in the drawers.

'Look at this, Johnny.' It was a small notebook with names and contacts next to them. 'See – that's the chief of police I told you about. And these are quite large sums of money next to his name and they're all at monthly intervals. That's odd, don't you think?'

'Was she blackmailing them then?' I said lightheartedly.

Serge looked again at the book and then very seriously said, 'I think you might be right, Johnny. And there are other names here, too, with regular payments each month.'

'I was only joking, Serge,' I said.

'Actually, no, I think you are right. These are all much more than her average charges.'

'How do you know? Were you a client of hers too then?' I quipped. I was trying to be funny and make him laugh, but instead he turned round defensively.

'I've never had to pay for it, Johnny.'

I'd hit a nerve. *What did he mean? Was he a faithful client?* I wondered. I decided to keep my mouth shut for a while and carry on sorting through her belongings.

'Hang on, here's Bruno's name again and his contact number,' said Serge. 'And the amount in monthly payments she was receiving from him. Surely she wasn't blackmailing him? Impossible! He would kill anyone who tried. He's totally ruthless. Or was it payments she was making to him? That seems far more likely. Mind you, when you saw what his vices were she must have had a pretty strong hold over him.'

There was the sound of a key turning in the front door lock and my heart missed a beat.

Claudette was about to walk in and catch us going through her things... I was sure of it. I held my breath as the door swung slowly back to reveal not Claudette... but Diddy. He stood staring at us for a moment as if totally surprised to find us in there. Then he walked into the middle of the room and looked around, as if searching for something. When he turned his eyes were haunted. He looked desolate and lost, like a little boy.

'I'm glad you're here, Diddy,' said Serge. 'We've just started sorting through Claudette's stuff. It's what she always said she wanted us to do when she went.'

Diddy walked around as if in a dream and sat down heavily on the chaise longue, staring into space.

Serge went over to him. 'Come on, the sooner we get this lot sorted the better. I was just telling Johnny, some of this stuff's worth a fortune. We were looking at all her expensive handbags stashed away; they must have been *cadeaux* from her rich clients. She certainly knew...'

'*Ta gueule!*' Diddy shouted (Shut your mouth!). He jumped up. 'Leave her things alone!' He was shaking with anger. His face crumpled and he slumped back down, sobbing with his face in his hands.

Serge looked at me, surprised. He mouthed '*Quoi?*' (What?) to me. The penny dropped. Serge made a silent 'Oh!' and knelt down, putting his arm round his son. 'It's all right, Diddy, I understand. She had a good life.'

Diddy wasn't listening. 'She was special... she understood... she was like a friend and a mother,' he choked out. He looked up. His eyes were wet with tears. He turned to Serge. 'She didn't smother me like my mum did. All my life she overwhelmed me with her love and tried to make me fill the gap you left. Claudette wasn't like that, she didn't want anything, she didn't demand my love. She just liked my company.'

Serge's eyes widened. He hadn't expected this outburst.

'*Maman* made me the centre of everything. It was unbearable... I couldn't do anything unless she was involved... it was too much... I had to get away. I was never allowed to be myself. That's the reason I came down here to find you. I thought you might be different... put things right.'

Serge was at a loss. He patted Diddy, trying to comfort him.

'I understand,' he said. 'I'm sorry I wasn't there for you when you were growing up.'

'Sorry? You're sorry! Where were you when I needed you? I needed to be protected from all that mollycoddling. If you had been there, we would have been a proper family and I could have been free to be a son, not a substitute partner to fill Mum's life up.'

Serge reddened. He tried to speak but nothing came out.

There was an awkward silence.

'Look, maybe I ought to be going,' I said. 'I didn't know Claudette that well.'

'No, it's OK,' said Diddy. 'Maybe you can understand how I felt growing up without a dad.'

I didn't know what to say. My dad used to beat me when I was a kid and I always breathed a sigh of relief when he went out. Life was much more bearable when he wasn't around.

'Claudette was good fun... we had a laugh... she was my best friend. She made life simple and I've never had that. My life has been a nightmare. I had to live with hidden secrets and lies. Claudette helped me, she really did. She told me about her life and I told her about mine.'

I caught Serge's eye and nodded to him to come in the other room.

'Maybe now's not a good time to do this,' I told him quietly. 'Diddy's really upset. He needs some time alone with his memories of Claudette. He's mourning her. It's hard for him.'

'Well, I had no idea he felt like that about her,' whispered Serge. 'They got on well together, I knew that much... but all

SON OF SERGE BASTARDE

that stuff about his mum and how Claudette was so special to him... I had no idea. I'm quite shocked really.'

'Let's give him some space,' I said. 'We can make a start clearing up tomorrow, can't we?'

'I suppose,' said Serge. 'Here, you don't think I was a bad father do you, Johnny? I mean, I didn't even know he was born till he turned up looking for me. And my poor Adrien – will he feel like that? How could we have been a proper family if I didn't know I had one?'

'You couldn't,' I said. 'If you'd known about him, you'd have been a proper dad. Don't beat yourself up, Serge. Look how you're trying to make it up to him now. It wasn't your fault.'

He looked relieved. As if I'd lifted a weight off him.

'OK, we'll leave him here in peace and make a start tomorrow,' said Serge. 'And thanks, Johnny...'

'For what?'

'For reassuring me... for telling me I'm not a failure as a father. It upset me when Diddy told me off like that... it really hurt!'

We went back into the living room where Diddy was still sitting, gazing into space. 'I'm seeing Johnny off,' said Serge. 'I'll leave you alone for a while.' Diddy half turned in acknowledgement and then looked away. We went out, pulling the door shut quietly behind us.

'I'll go back in a while and take him out for a drink,' said Serge, 'take his mind off it.'

'I think it'll take more than a drink to do that, Serge,' I said.

198

'Maybe so... that's a whole can of worms opened up in there now. Not sure if I'm up to all this, Johnny.'

'You'll be fine,' I reassured him, giving his arm a squeeze.

I left and as I glanced back at him standing all alone in the darkened hallway he looked almost as lost as Diddy did. *What a mess, the pair of them,* I thought to myself as I ran down the stairs.

Outside, as I was leaving, something made me turn round and look up. Claudette was standing at the window, gazing down at me. I'd been right all along. She was still haunting the place. We stared at each other, she gave me a little smile... then she turned and disappeared back into the room.

17

SANDY BEACHES
AND STRAW PARASOLS

I turned off the busy motorway and headed down the deserted winding road towards the Atlantic coast. It was early on Sunday morning and I was off to the *brocante* market held every month throughout the summer at Hendaye on the Spanish border.

The coast road that leads down to Hendaye is awe inspiring. As I negotiated the bends I glanced down over rugged cliffs to rocky beaches pounded by luminescent foaming surf. It always reminded me of a scene from the over-the-top Roger Corman horror film *The Raven*, starring Vincent Price.

The market is held in an airy square between the sea and an inland marina off the estuary. I checked my watch; it was ten past six as I parked my van on the promenade road.

The fair organiser hadn't turned up yet so I decided to get some fresh air and take Buster for a walk along the beach, which was deserted apart from the neat rows of Caribbean-style straw parasols. It was late July, and later, when the sun came up, it would be thronged with holidaymakers. As soon as I unclipped Buster's lead he charged off, his short legs going like the clappers. All our Staffs had loved the seaside and Buster was no exception. I watched him in the distance, barking excitedly at the waves as I walked along feeling the soft sand between my toes. It took me back to the holidays we had in Devon when I was a kid, me and my brother playing on Woolacombe Sands. My dad had decided he wanted to get out of insurance and start a pig farm. We visited remote Devon farms trying to find a suitable place to buy. I loved the idea.

My dad changed out there in the country. He wasn't his normal irritable self. He was relaxed and, dare I say it, fun. If he was going to become a farmer, I wanted to be there alongside him, working with animals. In the end it never happened. My mum hated the thought of being buried in the middle of nowhere and finally managed to talk him out of it and we stayed where we were, safe in the suburbs.

In the distance I saw two figures with a dog coming towards me. I worried for a moment, that Buster might come back and cause trouble, but he was too busy barking at the waves. The couple drew closer and I could make out a woman and a young girl. The dog, a big German shepherd, was running along ahead of them. He suddenly swerved and made a beeline for me. He was one of those big powerful dogs with a thick mane of dark fur. He came bounding towards me and jumped up on his hind legs. For a heartbeat I felt a stab of fear. His panting jaws were up by my face. But he simply bounced his front paws on my chest, then dropped back down on all fours and went leaping off, back to his charges. I knew exactly what this was. Maybe I should have felt annoyed that such a large dog was not under the control of his owners, but I didn't, I was impressed. This intelligent dog was protecting his vulnerable mistresses. The woman apologised for his behaviour as they came past, but I assured her it was perfectly all right and that they couldn't be in safer hands (or paws). Buster, on the other hand, was the type of dog that wanted to make friends at all costs. He was more of a playboy than a guard dog but I loved him anyway. I crossed to where Buster was still barking at the waves and put him back on the lead.

I could see a group of *brocanteurs* gathered round the market entrance and hurried across the road to join them. The market here was independently run by a woman called Françoise and her husband Jean-Pierre who worked together (as Helen and I did). Jean-Pierre let his wife do all the organising (as Helen does for me). They hired the square from the local commune through the mayor's office, arranged all the advertising and collected a fixed rate from the *brocanteurs* as rent for their stands. But some of the dealers gave her a hard time and were quite rude if they couldn't have their favourite place on the market. Françoise was an

Anglophile and always allocated me a spot overlooking the marina where all the millionaires' yachts were moored – I never had anything to complain about.

I was starting to unload my stock when I spotted Serge and Diddy arriving late as usual. I had asked Françoise if she could save the stand next to me for them and she'd hesitated. 'They were late last month,' she said, 'and that son of Serge's is really quite rude.'

'He won't be this time,' I assured her. 'I'll have a word with him.'

'Very well, John, but if he's difficult today I won't be giving them a place in future.'

Serge was pulling up by the marina. I waved and went across to him.

'I've fixed up for you to stall out next to me,' I explained. I was feeling pleased to be able to arrange something for him for a change. He leant out the van window, bleary-eyed.

'Thanks, Johnny, I feel like a zombie – I've not had a wink of sleep.' He nodded towards Diddy, who was slumped back in the seat beside him fast asleep with his mouth open. 'He's dead to the world. We've been sorting through the stuff in Claudette's flat all night. Diddy found it hard – it's been hell.'

He climbed out, opened the back of his van and began setting up his parasols. The sun was coming up, shining through the bristling masts of the hundreds of expensive yachts moored in the marina. Sandwiched between the beach and the blue of the estuary, this was a heavenly place

SON OF SERGE BASTARDE

to work. There was only one small drawback – across the river in Hondarribia in Spain they had built an airport and the planes took off regularly over the town, climbing with a jet roar into the clear blue skies. The French would never allow such a thing but in Spain 'anything goes'.

Serge began unloading huge armfuls of designer clothes which he hung on metal display stands like the ones they use in shops. They were the gowns from Claudette's flat and out here in the morning sunshine they looked very impressive. He wheeled out a large antique cheval mirror and positioned it where the customers who would want to try on these wonders could see themselves. Diddy had woken up and was standing around with his hands in his pockets, looking miserable. Serge set him to work arranging Claudette's huge collection of handbags and shoes in several big cardboard boxes. A few early-morning bargain hunters were beginning to drift into the market but they were all walking straight past my stand, drawn towards Serge's expensive-looking display. I realised straight away that it had been a bit of a mistake to have arranged a place for him next to my stand. As soon as the people checked out the prices they couldn't believe their eyes and a crowd of eager women began to swarm round. I pushed through and examined the tags. Serge had priced the stuff very reasonably, maybe even too cheaply. Some of the women were beginning to lose it, grabbing at the handbags and dresses, trying to squeeze their feet into Claudette's shoes.

Serge strolled over, looking pleased as Punch. 'Think I'm going to have a good day today, eh Johnny?' He was chuffed. 'You know, I forgot to tell you – I finished reroofing that big old Basque house with a bit of help from Diddy and Bruno was pleased with the job. Looks like I won't be walking around on crutches after all.' I was glad to hear it. I promised myself in future I would try to stay as far away from Bruno as possible. Serge pointed across the road. 'I've fixed up a curtain in the back of my van so my charming lady customers can try on the dresses in private. I've got it all worked out.'

Diddy was serving a large woman in a bright floral print dress. She bought a crocodile skin handbag and as he went to wrap it up another woman grabbed at it, insisting she had seen it first.

The large woman pushed her and a heated argument began. Diddy looked peeved and upset. He normally enjoyed a good catfight.

'We're going to sell out at this rate,' said Serge. 'Luckily I've got a whole lot more. Claudette was a right hoarder, God bless her.' A young woman came over with a Biba dress. She wanted to try it on so Serge took her across the road to his van, lifted the curtain and helped her in. He looked over and winked at me. He was enjoying this.

I returned to my stand. It was a bit depressing watching the mad rush round Serge's but a Spanish couple were examining an oak student's desk I had for sale. They said it would suit their son, who was going to college. These little honey-coloured desks made in the early part of the twentieth century fit snugly against a wall and are ideal for a bedroom or small study. That's why the Spanish, who have a taste for English furniture, love them and as they're not too expensive they sell well. I knocked a little bit off the price and they bought it. As I helped them with it across the road to where their four-wheel drive was parked, I heard a loud yell and Serge came running across the road, waving madly at me.

'Johnny! Johnny!' He was beside himself. 'I've just seen Angelique!'

I put down the desk. 'No! Where?'

'She was on the deck of one of those yachts in the marina! It was her, she had my little Adrien with her!'

'Are you sure, Serge?' I said.

'It was her all right. Look after my stand, please,' he pleaded. 'Diddy's throwing a moody. I'm going over to see her.'

And before I could answer he was back across the road, running along the marina.

I helped load the desk into the couple's car and went back over to his stand, which was swarming with women excitedly examining dresses, shoes and handbags. Diddy was sitting in a canvas chair staring into space, ignoring them. Buyers were frantically looking around for someone to pay for their purchases. Gowns were strewn about and it was futile trying to rearrange them on the hangers and take money at the same time. When you get a buying frenzy there's not much you can do but go with the flow. A crowd always attracts inquisitive customers who think they might get a bargain as well, and Claudette's clothes were driving them crazy. Luckily Serge had priced up his stock. By law, in France traders are obliged to display prices on all items. This discourages the dubious practice of sizing up the prospective customer and, if they seem rich, bumping up the price. Serge told me he had been inspected by the gendarmes before and fined on the spot for every piece not carrying a price tag. Since then he'd been religious about pricing up.

Soon I had a thick wad of euro notes stuffed into my bumbag. I looked across at the marina hoping to see Serge but he had disappeared. There were a few customers round my stand too and I couldn't afford to lose sales. I was about to tell Diddy to take over when someone tapped me heavily on the shoulder. I turned and looked straight into the face of Bruno the Basque. His eyes were blazing.

'What's this?' he demanded gruffly. He was holding a leather bag.

My heart sank.

'It's a good quality handbag,' I said, giving a strained smile.

'Where did you get this?' He looked about to explode. I felt a rush of fear. What was this all about?

'It's one of S-serge's, I'm just m-manning his stand for a m-minute.' I was actually stuttering.

'Where is the little toad?' he snarled.

'He's just nipped over the road, he won't be long,' I blurted out.

Bruno opened the clasp on the bag and looked inside. I couldn't believe my eyes when he drew out a slip of paper adorned with neat copperplate handwriting – it was the handbag that Bruno had given Claudette and the paper had his own name on it, with his sexual proclivities!

Why on earth hadn't they taken all those pieces of paper out? Bruno's eyes widened, he crumpled up the slip and thrust it deep into his pocket. He looked at me, sizing up my reaction. He wasn't sure if I had put two and two together.

'We can do you a good price on that one if you're interested, Bruno,' I said, feeling somewhat lightheaded.

He ignored me. 'Tell Serge I want to see him,' he said, tucking the bag under his arm. With that he turned on his heel and strode off across the market.

I returned to my stand feeling sick. I wasn't even worried whether Diddy was taking care of their business. My mind was whirling. I watched the crowd of women round Serge's stand looking desperately for the stallholder, clutching money in their hands. I wondered when Serge would reappear and if he'd found Angelique and his little Adrien. Then I spotted him in the distance, walking slowly. His body language said it all. I felt really sorry for him. He shuffled up to me, ignoring the mayhem on his stand.

'I was sure it was her,' he said dejectedly.

'But it wasn't?'

'I don't know. I went from boat to boat asking if anyone knew anything and I drew a total blank. No one knew a thing. Maybe I imagined it, Johnny.'

'Your stuff's been selling well,' I said. I pulled out the wodge of euros and handed them to him. He didn't look interested as he normally would have done.

'Thanks, Johnny, I appreciate it. Diddy's an emotional wreck since Claudette died. I can't rely on him for anything.'

I had to tell him about Bruno and what had happened. He really wasn't in the mood to listen but he needed to know. I explained about the handbag and Bruno finding the note with his name on it.

'*Merde!* I must have overlooked that note. Diddy swore he'd taken them all out. What did Bruno say?'

'He told me to tell you he wants to see you.'

He rolled his eyes heavenward. 'That's all I need! The boy's useless – fancy leaving it. And why the hell did it have to be Bruno's? What have I done to deserve all this, Johnny?'

I didn't know what to say. Things appeared to be going from bad to worse. But I had other things keeping me awake at night. Hovering in the back of my mind was the thought that Helen and I were going to have to up sticks soon. That was if we could find a place where we wanted to move.

18

LORENZO AND HIS BROTHERS

A few days later Serge phoned to tell me Lorenzo the *gitan* had offered him first refusal on some stuff from a house clearance. '*C'est génial.* Since all that business at Ousse-Suzan I'm suddenly his oldest pal.' He appeared to have got over the disappointment of not finding Angelique at Hendaye. Maybe all the money he made on the contents of Claudette's wardrobe had helped.

'Have you heard anything from Bruno?' I asked.

'Ah, Bruno the Basque.' He gave a little chuckle. '*Pour lui la mayonnaise a tourné.*'

'How do you mean?' He sounded a bit like a villain in a James Bond film.

'Never you mind, Johnny. Trust me, *pas de soucis.* Listen, Diddy's taken the van. He's out visiting his daughter and he's going to come over to Lorenzo's later. Could you do me a favour and come and fetch me? I'm sure there will be a few bargains for you and Helen as well.'

I said we would and Helen and I picked him up at Biarritz and drove to where Lorenzo lived in the Landes forest a few kilometres south of where the fair was held. We could smell the nearby *papeterie* (paper factory). It gave off an all-pervading stench, filling the air with reeking smoke that billowed from a tall chimney.

'A mate of mine lives in a small town right next to one of these factories and he swears there is no smell even when I tell him it stinks,' said Serge.

We passed through a village and I pulled up near the church to see if I could find someone to ask the way. It was quiet, hardly a soul about, like many French villages round here. A woman was walking a small dog on a lead and when I drew up alongside she came over to see what I wanted. Buster tried to climb over me to poke his head out the window and see her dog. When we first moved to France we were surprised how everyone in the rural villages knew everyone who lived in the vicinity. So I was expecting a positive response, but not the one I got. When I asked her if she knew where Lorenzo lived she looked at me as if I'd said a dirty word. She went to turn away, and then, thinking better of it, waved her hand, indicating the road ahead.

'Carry on for a couple of kilometres past the paper factory and it's on the right-hand side,' she said. 'A human rubbish tip parked on a mess of *ferraille*... you can't miss it.'

'What was that all about?' asked Helen. 'Lorenzo's not that popular round here, is he?'

'I don't see why,' said Serge. 'He and his family have settled near the town. He's a man of property and his family have built houses and installed mobile homes. His kids go to the local school, they're part of the community.'

'Is the stigma of being a *gitan* that hard to break?' I said.

'It depends,' said Serge. 'I know some people who are accepted and some who are not.'

A bit further on we came to a turn-off up a mud road leading to a group of houses and mobile homes. There were flowering shrubs in wooden tubs round the entrance and as we drove up the drive we were greeted by the sound of children's laughter. On a trampoline set up in the garden behind one of the houses a boy of about ten was bouncing in the air, while a small girl and boy shouted encouragement. Another boy on a chopper bike saw us arrive and rode past smiling good-naturedly. They were fascinated to see Buster staring out at them with his tongue hanging out.

Looking across through a gap between the houses and the mobile homes I could see the *ferraille* (scrap iron) the woman had mentioned. Parked in a field were old tractors, bits of abandoned cars, a couple of big iron water tanks, and mountains of rusty metal. But the houses and mobile homes were immaculate, with hanging baskets of geraniums and brightly painted doors and shutters. There was a tough-looking old lady dressed in black sitting in a deck chair on a veranda. She was watching us, interested to see who was arriving.

The doors on a nearby prefabricated concrete barn slid back and a big man came out dressed in blue overalls, wearing thick leather gauntlets and a welder's mask. He removed the mask and there was Lorenzo, his face wet with perspiration. He saw us and came over, wiping his face with a handkerchief. The woman from the veranda joined him and he introduced her to us – she was his mother. She gave us each a hug in turn and then Lorenzo invited us to follow him into the barn. There was a pungent sulphurous smell in the air. He waved towards where he had been working, welding a large metal table. To one side was a metal chest with riveted drawers. Helen recognised what they were and confided to me, 'He's making industrial-style furniture – very trendy at the moment.' She was impressed.

Serge looked confused. He gave me a secret look and pulled a face. He didn't understand what was going on here.

Lorenzo noticed the reaction. 'You think I'm crazy, eh Serge? I'm not surprised. Everyone thought I was mad when I started. My sons made fun of me but they soon changed their minds. I sold a big metal table like this for a small fortune to a dealer in Paris last month.'

Serge examined the table and pulled out one of the drawers on the chest. There was a din outside and Syd and Fabio arrived, hefting a large metal water tank which they slammed down against the barn wall.

'Since I found out there's a big demand for this furniture and I started making it I realised I couldn't get enough heavy sheet metal any more,' explained Lorenzo. 'We're running out already and it's the devil of a job to find the good old stuff. They stopped making metal tanks a while ago. It's all plastic now, and even though we've collected old scrap metal over the years there's not enough left to meet the demand. It's always the way, isn't it?'

'Where's Diddy?' asked Fabio.

'He's coming over in my van,' said Serge. 'I'll give him a ring and check he's not got lost.'

Lorenzo showed us round the back of the barn where they had stacked up all the stuff from the house clearance. He pulled back a heavy-duty *bâche* (tarpaulin) to reveal dismantled armoires and beds, and on a trestle table chandeliers, lights, paintings, ornaments and kitchenalia.

'Take your pick.' He made a magnanimous gesture. 'There are some nice bits here. We can come to an arrangement on the prices afterwards. But don't worry, it's going to be a lot less than you'd normally pay at auction. I always give my friends a good deal.'

As we sorted through the pieces I looked up and noticed two teenage girls leaning against the wooden railings of one of the mobile homes. There was something about them that looked familiar. Where had I seen them before? They were dressed up to the nines, like they were off to a party. But clearly they weren't, they were just lounging about passing the time of day.

Lorenzo's mum had made herself comfortable in an old garden chair and was smiling at us indulgently as if to encourage us. Then it all came back to me: the old woman in black who had been shouting at Diddy at Ousse-Suzan and the pair of jailbait girls he had been chatting up. I had also seen him sneaking back to the van late that night. What had he been up to? I was pretty sure one or both of the girls had been involved in his shenanigans. And these were the same girls. I was sure of it. And Lorenzo's mum was the woman in black. She would recognise Diddy as soon as he turned up in Serge's van. I knew the older generation *gitans* put great store on a young girl's virginity. For a *gitan* girl to get a well-connected, respected husband she had to be 'pure' and have an unsullied reputation. That was why Lorenzo's mother had reacted so strongly against Diddy.

I had to tell Helen. She would know what to do. I took her to one side and began to explain the situation. She was fascinated. We looked over at the teenage girls.

'My God, they're really young,' she said. 'They must be under sixteen.'

'And their grandmother is determined to protect them,' I said. 'I don't think she'll be too pleased to see Diddy again.'

'She may well be too late,' said Helen. 'It's a bit like shutting the stable door after the horse has bolted. In their case they look a right pair of ravers.'

'Do you think I'd better let Serge know?' I said. 'He could ring Diddy and stop him.'

'Yes, be quick, he's on his way here.'

I pulled Serge to one side and explained why there could be trouble when Diddy turned up. He listened to me, nodding.

'I don't want to annoy Lorenzo just when it's all going so well,' he said. 'And I'm not shocked by what Diddy gets up to any more. You know he's already got a kid from some woman he knocked up. He just can't resist the temptation to *tremper son biscuit* [dip his wick].'

'Was that his little girl I saw with him at Soumoulou?' I asked.

'Yes, that's his little Floriana. She's totally out of control.'

'She did seem a bit of a tomboy.'

'Diddy can't be bothered to discipline her. He lets her run wild when he has her for the weekend. She's like him – off the rails.'

I didn't point out that this might apply in Serge and Diddy's case as well. Helen was signalling to me and pointing. A white van was arriving with Diddy behind the wheel. We were too late!

Diddy leapt out and waved. Syd and Fabio went over to greet him. Fabio slapped him on the back. They were pleased to see him. The three of them came across, laughing and joking. When the girls saw Diddy they too came hurrying over. They were squealing with delight.

Helen and I exchanged looks and tried to see how Lorenzo's mum would react. But she hadn't noticed and was leaning back on the garden chair in the sun. Now the girls were coming over holding on to Diddy's arms and she was beginning to show some interest. She peered at them, checking to see who had arrived.

'Uh-oh,' said Helen. 'That's done it.'

The old lady leant forward. She had recognised Diddy all right. Her expression was priceless... changing from mild interest to instant fury. She jumped up and headed for them, shaking her fist and screaming abuse. They saw her coming and Syd and Fabio tried to fend her off, but she grabbed one of the girls by the arm, pulling her away. The other girl tried to drag her back and they all began shouting insults at each other. The commotion brought Lorenzo out from the barn. He stood there amazed, as if he couldn't believe his eyes. He looked at us like we might know what was going on, but we shrugged, disowning it. His mum began shouting across to him, demanding he do something. Serge looked embarrassed.

Lorenzo picked up a heavy hammer and strode purposefully over to the big iron tank. He swung the hammer high and slammed it against the side again and again. The sound was deafening, reverberating like thunder. Everyone stopped in their tracks, swung round and looked in his direction. He stood with hammer in hand like some Old Testament patriarch and when he saw he had everyone's attention he spoke with authority in a low, controlled voice. He ordered his daughters indoors. They sloped off in silent acquiescence.

He turned firstly to Diddy. 'Out of respect to your father I'll say this once. Don't interfere with my girls!' When he turned to Serge his voice was like ice. 'We control our children... you control yours.'

Sheepishly, with heads bowed, we all got on with choosing our furniture.

19

HARES AND GINGERBREAD

It was still proving hard for me to cope with the thought of moving. I loved our old house and the land around it. It had a hold on me and didn't want to let me go, nor I it. So what if it was a bit primitive and I hadn't finished all the work and renovations I had planned? Whenever I stood outside the back door and looked out over the fields across to the village I got a warm feeling. I felt I belonged here.

'Maybe it won't be so bad,' I kept saying to Helen. 'If we grew a tall hedge along the edge, we probably wouldn't see all the new houses.'

'Yes, but how are you going to feel with the fields gone? We'll be remembering how beautiful it was. It will never be the same again.'

I'd eventually come round to Helen's way of thinking. It had gone against the grain, but when it came down to it, as usual, she was right. When I managed to think rationally about it I could see how I would hate it once it all changed. We had decided this time we would try to find a house that needed hardly any work or renovation. As a drummer and a writer I made a lousy builder. I had enjoyed my foray into roofing, plumbing and electrical wiring, but if we could find a place that was habitable and restored, that would be ideal. And a proper bathroom would be nice, not just a bath in the kitchen where you could soak and drink a cup of tea and chat to someone cooking the dinner. I thought it was a great laugh but it was a bit embarrassing when we had guests who weren't so keen on the lack of privacy. Also, I hated to think what would happen if something went wrong and the wiring shorted out. I didn't want to be around when a professional electrician investigated my bodged work and began cursing me as 'that idiot cowboy'.

Helen had taken some flattering photographs of our house, barns and fields and given the details to several estate agents. We realised that no one English would want to buy an old farm in the country with a housing estate about to be built right next door to it, but as we were near Dax it might suit a French couple who wanted to commute to the town for work. We'd had several visits from people looking to buy but so far no offers.

Meanwhile, Helen had been visiting houses on her own, with the two of us returning later to any that might have potential. Buying a restored house in the Chalosse was proving to be too expensive for us. Inspired by our time spent at the Ousse-Suzan fair she began looking in the Landes forest and discovered it was a cheaper area. None of our French friends wanted to move there. Maybe it was too remote. They much preferred the rolling farmlands of the Chalosse or the Atlantic coast. And it didn't seem to appeal to many English people either. Living in the middle of a pine forest possibly wasn't the typical dream of a new life in France. It was much wilder than where we were now.

The Landes forest is massive, one of the largest in Europe. The population has more or less stayed at the same level for the past 150 years. It stretches inland from the Atlantic coast with its miles of sandy beaches and reaches right up to Bordeaux. It was originally a vast boggy moor (*la lande* means moor in French), unhealthy and inhabited by shepherds who walked about the swampy terrain on stilts tending their flocks. They elevated this stilt-walking to an art and it's still kept alive now by entertaining troupes of performers who give colourful exhibitions of their skills with long stilts strapped to their legs. Unsurprisingly, mosquitoes used to flourish in this wet area and there was malaria here a couple of hundred years ago. The people were sickly and undernourished with a low life expectancy. It was sometimes known as the 'French Sahara' and crossing the moor was dreaded by the pilgrims on the Camino de Santiago de Compostela (Way of St James) in medieval times, who reported they could 'find no bread, no meat, no fresh water'. It was Napoleon III who passed a law in 1857 ordering all the communes of Landes Gascony to drain the Landes and plant pine trees, which had the effect of making the land usable and rich. And today it is a vast shady pine forest populated by deer, wild boar, hare, badgers, foxes, polecats and pine martens. There is even supposedly a species of European wildcat similar to the one in the Scottish Highlands.

One of the estate agents, a sad-faced little man with a grey goatee beard, showed us pictures of several 'desirable properties'. He seemed like a sober, sensitive chap and we agreed to accompany him in his Renault Espace to visit them. This was a mistake. It broke our self-imposed rule of not travelling in cars with French drivers. When we first came to France we had given a lift to a neighbour who complained about our sluggish speed. 'You English, you care too much about life,' he observed. It was a criticism we were willing to accept. From experience we had learnt some time ago not to be passengers with French drivers in their cars. Our nerves weren't up to it. They drove far too fast and recklessly for our Anglo-Saxon sensibilities. Drive along most roads in France and you come across pitiful little bunches of plastic flowers, memorials to the victims of fatal accidents. In some regions they have been running a scheme to illustrate the number of fatal accidents on especially dangerous roads. For every death they place a black cut-out of a human figure with a bright painted lightning flash on the head to indicate where the fatality occurred and smaller ones to denote children. It is chilling to see the senseless loss of life so vividly depicted when you pass one after another of these cut-out figures on a road that has witnessed many fatalities. I was told by a young French friend learning to drive that his instructor insisted he 'drive with punch'. I felt like asking him, what about Judy? But there would have been no point (they don't have Punch and Judy in France, but they do have Le Guignol, which is very similar). Any dawdling by drivers is considered bad form and it is important not to hold up other motorists as they might become irritated and start hooting and gesticulating madly.

No sooner had we fastened our seat belts than the estate agent floored the accelerator and we were pinned back in our seats like astronauts on a moon launch.

We tore out of town and up a road that ran straight through the forest with the trunks of pine trees flashing past and the dappled sunlight shining down through the high branches. A speck appeared in the distance. We found ourselves hazarding a guess as to what sort of vehicle it might be. The road we were on was straight but not very wide. As the speck grew larger we saw with horror that it was a lorry, and as it loomed larger still that it was loaded up with massive pine trees, probably headed for the nearest wood yard or paper mill. Our driver appeared unperturbed, hugging the centre of the road, refusing to pull over. At the last possible moment, with a quick flick of the wheel, he dodged the oncoming juggernaut, skidding and bucking along the dirt verge, leaving us with our hearts in our mouths. We endured several close calls like this, visiting uninspiring houses tucked away in the deepest parts of the forest. And we began to long for it to stop. But our man pressed on, determined to find something to our taste. He couldn't bear to lose a possible buyer for his enormously inflated fee.

It was late afternoon and we had just about lost hope when he swung off the main road up a winding dirt drive and pulled up outside a pink-walled, half-timbered house with sea-blue shutters and a studded oak door. It was like an Arthur Rackham illustration of a gingerbread house from a Brothers Grimm fairytale, or maybe Snow White's cottage. I looked at Helen in disbelief. Were we dreaming? Was this a figment of our imagination? Would the Seven Dwarfs suddenly appear?

Our man got out of the car and was checking through a bunch of heavy iron keys, searching for the one to open the door. We looked around, enchanted. There was an old mossy stone well with a wooden bucket for drawing the water. The house itself had a higgledy-piggledy tiled roof above the *colombage* (half-timbering), which was set into the pink stucco walls and curved into strange, compelling shapes like the sides of a galleon. It was captivating. We didn't need to think about it. We were smitten!

'Come on in and have a look inside.' The agent had opened the front door and was beckoning to us. He began throwing back the shutters to let the light in. It was as if we had entered a bygone age. We were standing in a quaintly decorated kitchen with a tiled floor and pink painted beams from which cast-iron pots were suspended in even rows. Against the walls stood a pair of mellow walnut-wood buffets stacked with Samadet-inspired faience plates (glazed earthenware decorated with opaque colours) and under the window there was a long rustic table ideal for preparing or eating meals at. Everything appeared to have been carefully and tastefully chosen to enhance the character of the house. The living room had more oak beams, limed walls and an open *cheminée* (fireplace) with worn-smooth old elm seats pushed up close to sit near the fire and toast your toes.

'It was originally living quarters for *resiniers*,' he said. 'They collected resin by making cuts in the trunks of pine trees and bleeding the resin into earthenware pots.'

Whoever had restored this old cottage knew what they were doing. It even had a proper finished bathroom with a bath, basin, bidet and shower. Oh joy of joys! This was real luxury!

But could we afford it? It seemed almost too good to be true, as if it had been waiting empty for us deep in the forest. There must be a catch. Was it owned by a wicked witch or a goblin with an unpronounceable name? Did we have to guess his name to have a stab at buying the place?

'It's owned by a very nice German couple,' said the agent. 'They use it as a summer residence.'

So that was why it was so well restored. The Germans are good at retaining original features and have a knack with country cottages and wood. It turned out that although the price they were asking was a bit of a stretch for us, if we managed to sell our old place we might be able to manage it. On the way back to his office the agent discussed the technicalities and said the German couple were due to visit the following weekend. He could arrange for us all to meet up. That's if we liked the property and wanted to make an offer. We did, we said, and we would. We were trying not to get too excited.

The next day we came back on our own with Buster sitting in the back and drove around, checking out the area. We have moved a few times and had a procedure we tried to follow when we were looking to buy a place. On the first visit if you fall for a house, you tend to miss things, especially if you are charmed by it. It's best to come back at different times of the day without an agent if possible, to get the real feel of the place. You never know, you might turn up a minus you had overlooked, such as a noisy road, a polluting factory or a homicidal neighbour who keeps pigs.

We parked at the top of the drive, clipped Buster's lead on his leather harness and walked down to the house, looking around, drinking in the atmosphere. The tall forest pines ran down to the edge of the grounds, giving way to stately oaks and various exotic trees that had been planted in the clearing. The agent had said the German couple were keen gardeners who spent their holidays working here. They seemed to have transformed this little corner into a walk in the Black Forest.

There was a movement near some rhododendron bushes under the big oak trees. We watched as a large hare hopped out into the open. He was big, much larger than a rabbit, with long ears and a head that had an almost skull-like quality. Hares are embedded in folk myths from cultures all over the world. We had never seen one so close as this before. He stopped, stood up on his hind paws and turned to look straight at us. Buster stiffened, straining at his lead, but the hare wasn't frightened. He watched for a moment, then dropped back on all fours and loped back through the bushes. It was thrilling. His appearance added to the absolutely magical feeling the house gave us. We loved it!

We rang the estate agent and told him we wanted to make an offer. He said he would pass it on to the German couple. Later he got back to us. They had accepted our offer and we arranged to meet them that Sunday.

The studded oak door was opened by a giant of a man in khaki shorts wearing a pink T-shirt that bore the legend 'Onwards Go in a Frostily Direction' on the front in green letters. His hair was cropped short, shaved up the sides and he had a small, square moustache.

Oh dear, I thought... *unfortunate moustache!*

'Hello, pleased to meet you.' He shook my hand and almost broke my knuckles with a macho squeeze. I hate it when men do that. It seems to be the antithesis of a friendly greeting. He said his name was Berthold and introduced his wife, Frieda. She stepped forward and gave us both kisses on our cheeks. She was blonde, ample-bosomed and wore a tasteful floral print dress. They took us on a guided tour of the house, which they proudly announced was being featured in the next edition of the French interiors magazine *Maison et Jardin*. They were ecstatic about this. So why were they selling then, we asked.

'It is too much for us now, we are getting old,' Berthold confided. 'We don't have time to keep the garden nice.' He explained to me that they had had a lot of trouble with 'the Seven Sleepers'.

'They build their liddle nests in the loft and make a horrible smell.' He took me out to his workshop and opened a cupboard filled with strange looking intricate wire traps. 'We catch them and take them deep into the forest and let them go,' he explained. 'It is *verboten* to kill them.'

I wanted to know more about these 'Seven Sleepers'. I had never heard of them.

'Ya, you call them Seven Sleepers in English,' he said. 'They are liddle rodents that sleep seven months of the year. The Romans used to eat them. You must know this word.'

Ah! He meant dormice.

'We don't call them Seven Sleepers,' I said.

'Ah no, you do,' he insisted.

I decided it was a waste of time to argue about it. *I'll dump those traps,* I thought, *as soon as we move in.* Although we had been 'townies' just like them, living in the French countryside had altered our view. We found the idea of cuddly, furry little rodents living in the loft quite appealing. We had had swarms of rats at harvest time in Portugal so dormice held no fears for us.

I was amazed at how tidy his workshop was, thinking about the mess mine was in. I'm always impressed by people who keep their things neat and promise myself I'll follow their example and be like that in future, but somehow I never manage it. Berthold took me up into the loft to see where the Seven Sleepers had been making their nests. He said he had removed all the loft insulation because it smelt bad. I was thinking we would have to put a load more in for us and the dormice. We would be living here all year round and the Landes can get very chilly during the short winter.

Berthold and Frieda were pleased we were buying their house but mistakenly believed we were keen gardeners like them. They had passed so many happy hours working in the garden, they said, and spent a good two hours telling us what we had to do and in what season.

'Everyone has been so kind and welcoming to us here,' Frieda said, her eyes filling with tears. I was surprised. This was the total opposite from my perception of how Germans are generally received here in France. Mr Leglise, our neighbour, often made disparaging remarks to me about the Germans. '*Les Bosch* occupied us during the war and now we're in the EU they're just coming in and buying us out and acting like *aristos*,' he moaned. I felt he was qualified to make this complaint. He lost his only son in the army during World War Two. Considering this, his reaction was mild.

The so-called Franco-German alliance doesn't really give the true picture. I hadn't realised just how the Germans were viewed by the ordinary country folk in France until we borrowed a friend's German-registered VW camper for a couple of weeks. The reception we received from our local supermarket petrol station was cold to say the least, and the looks from passers-by were decidedly frosty. In my teens I toured Germany with my band, Lester Square and the GTs, which subsequently broke up over there and I ended up, at one stage, working in the cloakroom of a club in Münster. I had made friends with the young drummer who worked in the club and spent many a happy hour hanging out with the resident group. The drummer's name was Udo Lindenberg and he went on to become one of the most celebrated rock stars in Germany. When I was handing over coats at the end of an evening, half-cut middle-aged German clubbers would embrace me when they discovered I was British, insisting, 'We didn't want to fight you English, you are like us... we never meant to go to war with you.' And I had to admit they had a point. Germans are like us. We understand the German Anglo-Saxon mindset more than the Gallic one. It is much closer to ours. The Saxons were Germanic peoples who invaded England and merged with the Angles and Jutes to become the Anglo-Saxons, so it's hardly surprising we get on.

'It is a little paradise here,' said Frieda.

'It's so hard to leave this wonderful idyll,' said Berthold.

Frieda was crying and even Berthold wiped away a tear. I decided they must have done something right to have won over their French neighbours. They were a kindly couple. Perhaps the Franco-German alliance in the EU had forced the French to view the Germans in a new light.

As we drove off through the pines I looked back and saw the pair of them standing outside their house, waving us goodbye.

'What do you think?' I asked Helen.

'We can move straight in, they've done all the work.'

'All we've got to do is sell our place,' I said.

'Don't be so pessimistic,' she said. 'We'll sell it, wait and see. I've got a *prêt relais* lined up in the meantime. It'll give us two years to sell our place.'

'What if we don't sell it in two years?'

'Don't even think about it,' she said.

I wasn't that confident. Although I liked this house in the forest, I was daunted by the thought of moving and leaving a place I had grown so fond of and all the neighbours we liked. 'I'll miss Roland and Mr Leglise,' I said.

'There'll be other neighbours here and you can always go back and see our old friends, it's only a forty-minute drive away – not far.'

'I suppose,' I said.

But I had the same sad, lonely feeling I always had when I was about to leave somewhere. And I knew in my experience I tended not to go back once I left a place I loved.

20

EXQUISITE GOOD TASTE

'I'm fed up with all this scrabbling about selling bric-a-brac,' said Serge. 'It's a misery in this weather.' We were sheltering from the pouring rain under our *parapluie* (umbrella) hunched up in woollies and waterproofs at Anglet market near Bayonne, watching the wind catch the sheets of drizzle, spraying our tables, soaking our stock. It was cold and miserable and there wasn't a customer in sight.

A sudden strong gust of wind caught the *parapluie* so we had to grab the pole to stop it from going over.

'Anyway, I'm going to go upmarket,' said Serge, holding on grimly. 'I want to become a proper *antiquaire*, Johnny.'

I turned to look at him, surprised. It suddenly struck me as funny. I wanted to laugh, watching the rain dripping off the end of his nose. I thought he was joking but he was deadly serious. 'Yes, I think I'll book us into a *salon d'antiquités* and leave all this misery behind.'

Maybe he was right but I wasn't sure about it. Helen and I had taken stands at more upmarket fairs in England but so far we had never done a *salon* in France. The weather here was generally more conducive to open-air markets, but right now the idea was starting to appeal to me. *Salons* were normally held in halls, in the warm. The stands were expensive so you had to make several good sales just to pay your rent, the hope being that a richer type of customer would be attracted by the opulence of the antiques on offer. With a better-heeled class of clientele there was more chance of shifting several expensive pieces and making a bigger profit. That was the theory, anyway. Most *brocanteurs* I knew would never dream of risking their meagre earnings at a *salon* so I was surprised when Serge had mentioned it.

I thought he was just daydreaming but the following day he phoned to say he had booked a stand at a *salon* to be held in Rennes in the north of France and wanted us to share it with him and Diddy. The price was high but affordable when split between the two of us. It was a four-day fair and so we talked it over and decided we'd risk it. We would throw in our lot with Serge and Diddy and become 'big time antiques dealers'.

A month later Helen and I set off with Buster in the van for the *salon*, arriving late on Wednesday to discover to our horror that our cubicle had 'Bastarde & Fils' printed in big letters on a sign over it.

'I'm not standing under that all day,' said Helen. 'It's embarrassing. I don't care how big a deal this is.'

'He must have forgotten our half,' I said. 'He was very excited; he's probably always wanted a sign like that.'

'Yes, obviously I don't care about our name, it's just that name – "Bastarde and Son". It might as well say "Steptoe and Son"! Or better still, "Dick Emery and Son".'

We collapsed into hysterical laughter. What were we doing?

Looking around I was surprised to see most of the French dealers had already set up their stands, tastefully arranging them to resemble opulent rooms in expensive homes with valuable rugs and antique furniture softly lit with spotlights and table lamps, the walls bedecked with precious paintings.

'I hadn't imagined we'd need to bring our own lighting,' I told Helen. I felt discouraged as I began unloading our furniture, piling it up higgledy-piggledy.

'I don't know how I let Serge talk me into this – we're going to look like amateurs. The richos won't give our stuff a second glance.'

'Will you pull yourself together,' said Helen. 'Don't be so negative. You always get intimidated. I'll sort this out and make it look really nice.'

Under Helen's guidance we began arranging the stand and waxing and polishing some of the better pieces of English furniture we had brought with us. I was relieved to discover there were overhead spotlights available with a control panel and after a couple of hours' work our half of the stand began to look quite inviting. I moved a couple of spots to pick out the softly glowing pieces of polished furniture. Very classy! Helen had pulled it off, just like she said she would. And I had changed my mind. How could we fail to make a fortune?

'Still purveying tat to the peasants?' I looked up into the supercilious face of Lord Snooty.

'Algie!' I was pleased to see him, despite the arrogant comments. I was getting used to them, even finding them quite amusing. 'What are you doing here?'

'Oh, I always do the upper echelon antiques fairs; you get a much higher class of clientele.' He was wearing plus fours, a loud pair of golfing shoes and a tartan waistcoat set off with a Paisley pattern cravat and a tweed deerstalker. He looked like an eccentric lord. He was the French stereotype of a mad Englishman.

'I really can't believe you are sharing a stand with that little shyster,' he said, pointing at the 'Bastarde & Fils' sign. 'I'm surprised at you, Helen. I'd have thought you had better taste.'

Helen had taken one look at him and was suffering from a fit of the giggles. His outfit had got to her. She had set me off too and I was trying to control myself when I spotted Diddy wheeling a trolley stacked with cardboard boxes. Serge was walking majestically beside him, wearing an expensive-looking suit with the jacket draped round his shoulders, carrying a silver-topped lacquered cane in one hand. As he approached I could see he was even sporting a pair of long pointy-toed shoes, a style much favoured by all the *gitans*.

He must have sold a couple of his gold coins and was feeling flush.

'Talk of the devil,' said Algie waving his hand disdainfully, 'and his son!'

Serge greeted us warmly, shook our hands and kissed Helen. He indicated to Diddy where he should place the boxes in his half of the stand and began unpacking the contents. They unwrapped tissue paper to reveal a collection of Chinese porcelain and statuettes of dubious provenance.

'Oh dear, they look new to me,' Helen whispered. 'They're all repro.' We watched, open-mouthed. 'Are you allowed to sell copies at this fair?' Helen asked.

'*Quoi?* Helen, these are not copies, they are valuable, much sought-after Chinese antiques.' He produced a file and pulled out a sheaf of papers. 'Here are the authenticated certificates of guarantee signed by an expert.'

'Was that the same expert who sold them to you?' Helen asked dryly.

Algie picked up a porcelain figure of a dragon and examined it. '*C'est nul!*' (It's rubbish!) he told Serge, scornfully replacing it on the table. 'Where did you buy this lot Serge, GiFi? ('GiFi' is a cut-price chain of French stores.)

Serge waved the guarantees under his nose.

'If you need a signed guarantee to prove something is genuine, then it must be a fake,' said Algie. 'Everyone knows that, old chap.'

He was right about that. We had visited antiques fairs in Spain that had featured stands selling so-called ivory netsukes (miniature carved Japanese sculptures) and intricately decorated tusks and figurines which the besuited salesmen had insisted were hand-carved from million-year-old mammoths' tusks recently discovered in Siberia. They screened non-stop videos of explorers digging up the mammoth remains and issued signed certificates as to their authenticity. But they were unable to offer us any believable explanation as to who had carved these tusks and pieces of ivory so perfectly with such incredible artistic skill. It was obvious that they were in fact very well cast in resin to resemble ivory. It was a scam and no amount of signed certificates or videos would convince us otherwise. In fact, the better antiques fairs in Madrid and the larger Spanish towns had barred these dodgy dealers completely.

Serge was unmoved by Algie's comments. 'You think I'm an idiot, do you? That me and my son would sell fakes?'

Algie guffawed rudely. 'Yes on both counts, Bastarde.' He turned to us. 'I really don't know what you're doing sharing a stand with this pair of buffoons.'

I was embarrassed by his outburst. Maybe Serge had got it wrong but we certainly weren't about to join Algie in poking fun at him.

'We thought it might be nice to sell inside in the warm,' I said. 'It's all very swish, isn't it?'

'Well, at least you have some quite nice pieces of English furniture,' Algie conceded. 'You should do all right, but I can't say the same for Bastarde and son.' He went off, chuckling to himself.

Exhausted from unloading and setting up our stand we left Serge and Diddy to it, took Buster for a swift walk round the block and checked into our hotel for an early night in preparation for the days ahead. Hotels and restaurants in France are very dog friendly and we have always been allowed to take Buster up to our room. It's impossible to stop him jumping up on the bed with us so we cover it with a blanket specially brought for the purpose.

The following morning found us queuing up with the other dealers, waiting to get into the hall early and add the finishing touches to our stand. While Helen unpacked some quality 'smalls' (as we English dealers call anything for sale that is not actually furniture; the French call them *bibelots*) and positioned them on our polished desks and tables, I fiddled with the lighting panel and tried to create even more tasteful lighting effects, taking inspiration from Mr Repro at Dax, hoping to impress the rich discerning buyers who were bound to turn up in droves. Serge arrived late.

'Where's Diddy?' asked Helen.

'He's gone to see his mother,' said Serge.

Helen and I exchanged looks. His mother?

When the doors opened at nine we were disappointed that just a handful of visitors strolled in.

A little short man came up to Serge and pointed at his stock. 'Is this yours?'

Serge, all proud, thought he was an early customer. 'Yes, what are you interested in?'

'All of it,' said the man. Serge looked triumphant.

'You're going to have to remove it all,' said the little man. 'You can't sell reproductions at this fair.'

'They aren't reproductions,' spluttered Serge. 'Who are you?'

'I'm Monsieur Belland the expert,' said the little man. 'I'm here at the request of the organisers to make sure everything sold at this fair is a genuine antique. You can pack up all this Oriental stuff and get it off your stand.' Serge was speechless. 'I'll be back in half an hour and it had better all be gone or else you'll have to leave,' he said officiously, walking off.

Serge watched him go. He looked stunned.

'Il est fou ce Monsieur Belland!' (He's mad!) 'He can go to hell!' But after a few minutes he began to pack some of the Chinese figures back in their cardboard boxes. It didn't matter much as the fair was dead. A few people meandered slowly about from stand to stand but no one seemed interested in buying. By midday we were starting to wish we hadn't come at all. We stood around, bored, praying at least one customer would show some interest. If it went on like this, we were going to lose money. I was beginning to wish we'd stuck to the *brocante* markets. I was missing the parasol and the open air. Why had I let Serge persuade us to go 'upmarket'?

Monsieur Belland returned to check Serge was following his orders. When he had made sure all the reproductions had been removed he went off satisfied. But once he was out of sight Serge pulled out a couple of the boxes and began replacing some of the banned items. This made us laugh.

'You're wasting your time, Serge,' I said. 'Might as well leave them in their boxes – no one's selling a thing.'

'Don't worry, it'll probably pick up tomorrow,' he said hopefully.

After lunch we sat around in an empty hall. Algie came past, looking glum. 'It's a misery,' he said. 'I've been chatting to the other dealers. It's a dead loss. I shan't be coming back here again.'

Around five in the afternoon, however, there was a flurry of buyers and an elderly silver-haired gentleman and his blonde, younger wife took an interest in a Swiss Mermod Frères cylindrical musical box Helen had bought in England. It was an exquisite piece with intricate machinery. I love anything that produces music and this was brilliant. It was the first music box of its kind we had ever had and the six melodic airs it played evoked childhood memories. The problem with a valuable and comparatively rare item like this is what level should you set the price? As it was the first one to pass through our hands we were unfamiliar with its subtleties. Helen had done some research and had set what she thought was a reasonable price. The silver-haired gentleman appeared to be familiar with exactly how the box worked and was obviously an avid collector. He made an offer which was somewhat less than we were hoping for but which gave us a good profit and would more than pay for the cost of our half of the stand. We hesitated but as the fair had been dead so far we accepted. As I wrapped the box Algie appeared and watched over my shoulder. He asked how much we had sold it for and when I told him he looked jealous. He squinted at the couple and I panicked – I thought he might interfere and start chatting to them. But he sloped off with a sick expression on his face.

Serge sat with his head in his hands looking glum. 'I don't know what's happened to Diddy,' he said. 'I've been ringing him all day. He's ignoring me. I don't think he's suited to this game. He gets bored so easily.'

'I'm sure he's all right,' said Helen. 'You haven't really needed him yet, have you? Only when you have to pack up.'

The fair started to pick up on Sunday morning. More people began turning up to look at what was on offer. Serge carried on sneaking back his Chinese repro little by little, but it didn't help; people just ignored his stock.

'I can't believe this,' he said, growing visibly more depressed. 'I was sure I was onto a good thing with these Chinese antiques.'

'Good job you found those gold coins in that house,' I said, trying to cheer him up.

He leapt up, grabbed me by the arm and pulled me over to one side. 'For God's sake, don't ever mention that again, Johnny! It never happened!' He was hissing in a stage whisper.

'Sorry, Serge, I didn't realise.' What had possessed me to bring that up? Me and my big mouth.

Just before lunch Algie came over to see us. 'I've just sold a bronze ormolu clock for a small fortune, and I've got a rich picture dealer interested in one of my oil paintings,' he crowed. His whole attitude had changed from yesterday.

Serge was totally down in the dumps. 'Did you hear that Bastarde? A small fortune! How's the GiFi stuff going? Not so good, what?'

Serge ignored him. He shot us a pleading look. He still hadn't heard from Diddy. He kept making circuits of the other stands with a haunted expression on his face, hanging round the entrance waiting for Diddy. We invited him to join us for lunch. It wasn't a very tempting offer. We sat in a corner together in a typically English manner eating home-made sandwiches and sipping hot tomato soup from plastic cups while the other French dealers laid out banquets of food and wine on their tables.

Algie came over. 'Ooh, cream of tomato soup, delicious! I always bring several tins back with me from Blighty. You can't beat it, that great British taste.'

'This is French, actually,' said Helen. 'It's almost the same, but much nicer, not tinny tasting.'

'If you say so,' said Algie, looking dubious. 'Anyway, excuse me if I don't join you. I've made a killing this morning,' he boasted, 'so I'm off into town for a slap-up lunch with all the trimmings. I'll tell you all about it when I get back.'

'Don't bother,' said Helen.

'Are you sure you won't join me, Helen? Or are you happy to eat your picnic with this rabble?' He pointed at me and Serge.

'No thanks,' said Helen. 'Don't choke on a fish bone, will you?'

Algie loved this and went off guffawing loudly. He and Helen had a good line in Cockney banter going between them now.

Serge seemed pleased to sit with us and nibble at a sandwich. 'I haven't got much appetite,' he said pathetically. We watched a party of dealers nearby stuffing their faces, quaffing wine, laughing and generally partying it up. This made it worse somehow. They were so jolly it amplified how depressed Serge was.

After lunch Algie staggered back, sated and half cut. He flopped on a chaise longue on his stand and promptly fell asleep. Visitors making the rounds stared at him lying there with his mouth open like a fish. He wore black patent leather shoes with silver buckles, beige socks with purple garters, a white silk shirt with flouncy sleeves, his tartan plus fours and a brilliant black-and-yellow chequered waistcoat. Dressed as he was in such outlandish garb, he was like an actor in some strange costume drama.

As the afternoon wore on more buyers began to turn up. By teatime we had some good profit in hand. Serge had sold nothing, there was still no sign of Diddy and the fair was nearly over.

A middle-aged woman was hovering about looking at Serge oddly.

'Looks like Serge's luck's in – I think he's pulled,' I said to Helen.

The woman approached our stand tentatively. She drew closer to Serge, who was sitting staring forlornly into space.

'*Bonjour*, Serge,' she said softly, leaning in closer.

He glanced up and a look of recognition spread over his face. 'Anne-Marie?'

'*Oui, c'est moi.*'

We tried desperately not to stare.

'It's been a long time, Serge.' She hesitated and looked away.

Serge stood up and kissed her on both cheeks. 'It's good to see you,' he said and, looking around, 'Is Diddy with you?'

'No, I'm afraid not.' Anne-Marie looked at us, embarrassed.

'It's OK, these are my friends, Helen and Johnny,' he said, touching her arm.

We said 'hello' and went to leave, but Serge stopped us.

'No, please stay, this is Diddy's mother.' She smiled and we all sat down uneasily together.

'I need to tell you something, Serge,' she said. 'It's very hard for me.' She looked at us.

We got up to leave yet again and Serge stopped us.

'These are my closest friends,' he told her. 'You can speak freely in front of them.'

Helen and I felt uncomfortable. We held hands and Helen squeezed mine gently.

'Please go ahead, Anne-Marie,' said Serge. 'I'm very pleased to see you. I've enjoyed having Diddy working alongside me. He's a credit to you.'

Helen squeezed my hand again. I got the message. Had it been a pleasure?

'I didn't know he was with you,' said Anne-Marie. 'He left and didn't say where he was going. I know he's a man, but to me he's still a child, even though he's a father himself. I think that was what made him come and find you.'

Serge looked proud and beamed. 'I'm pleased he did,' he said. 'You know, Anne-Marie, if I had known I would have come back. I would have been a proper father to him. Why didn't you tell me about him?'

'Oh, Serge!' She was close to tears. 'You obviously love him. It's a really long story but, I'm so sorry to have to tell you... he's not your son.'

Helen and I froze.

'Sorry?' Serge repeated. 'Did you say NOT my son? What do you mean? He's just like me!'

Helen squeezed my hand again. Yes, he certainly was just like him!

'You must understand, Serge. It was very difficult for me. We were so young. There were so many problems,' said Anne-Marie. 'You went out a lot and then you were in the army. There was someone else... someone who was kind to me.'

'What do you mean kind?' said Serge.

'My parents put so much pressure on me to marry. And you grew more and more distant. And then you started going away, and the army... I was lonely.'

'So you had someone else? Who was it? Where is he now? Why does Diddy think I'm his father then?'

'It's complicated,' she said.

'Why? I don't understand. How do you know that he isn't mine and that he's this other man's? Presumably you were sleeping with us both!'

Helen was squeezing my hand tighter. We were both staring at the floor. We didn't know where to look.

'He couldn't bring Diddy up,' said Anne-Marie. 'We split up... he loved me, but he couldn't marry me or be a dad, it would have destroyed him. He wasn't that strong.'

'Just tell me who he is, for God's sake,' he pleaded.

She took a deep breath. 'It was Father Gregorie.'

Serge looked stunned.

'I went to him for all my problems... he helped me... and then we fell in love. He wanted to leave the church and marry me... but his faith was too strong. It's a small village. The scandal would have destroyed him... and I loved him so. I told everyone Diddy was yours. No one doubted it. When you didn't come back people were sympathetic, they felt sorry for me. It was the perfect solution. Diddy was accepted. I thought you might come back and we would be together again... but you never did. I gave up.'

'Oh, *formidable*!' said Serge. 'And would you have told me? Or would you have let me carry gaily on like a cuckoo bringing up someone else's child?' He stopped dumbfounded for a moment. 'Are you absolutely certain he's not mine?'

'Yes. I never thought he would come and find you,' said Anne-Marie.

'Yeah, well that's great!' snorted Serge. 'I have a son you know – a real one – and I've lost him, and now I've lost another. And where's Diddy now, anyway?'

'I told him and he's angry with me,' said Anne-Marie. 'He's gone away again. I thought he might have come here.' She looked around at the dealers packing up their stands.

'Well, you can't blame him for being angry,' said Serge. 'I'm angry... I'm hurt... I'm...' He was suddenly lost for words. He covered his face with his hands and slumped forward. Helen went to comfort him as Anne-Marie stood watching, helpless. 'I'm so sorry,' she said to me. Tears were streaming down her face. She looked around, lost.

Then she turned and walked straight off towards the exit. She didn't look back.

Serge stayed bent over, head in hands. We began packing up our things but he still didn't move.

'This is terrible,' said Helen. 'I think he's in shock. What are we going to do?'

'I think we might have to help him pack up his stock,' I said. 'He seems to have lost interest.'

As I loaded his Chinese porcelain into their cardboard boxes Serge sat as motionless as one of his reproduction statuettes. His silver-topped cane lay cast aside and kicked into a corner.

21

VIOLINS AND TEDDY BEARS

It was the monthly Soumoulou fair at the little village on the road to Tarbes not far from Lourdes, and I was setting up my stand on our regular pitch. I'd left Helen at home packing up boxes for our move. We hadn't seen or heard from Serge for some time, ever since the *salon d'antiquités*. He didn't answer my calls and I'd been to his flat several times but there was no one there – he'd disappeared again. I had arrived at the fair at about 6 a.m. as usual to make sure I could park my van easily. The stands were so close together that if you arrived late it was impossible to drive up the narrow aisles and squeeze your vehicle into its allotted space. The man who ran the Soumoulou market was a bearded giant, a stickler, insisting the market should run like clockwork. He was '*sérieux*' as the French like to say, to indicate he was professional and treated his job with the import it deserved. Consequently all the dealers arrived at the market at a ridiculously early hour to get parked and had to hang around in the dark waiting for it to grow light and the first customers to arrive.

I greeted and shook hands with a *gitan* dealer who was known by everyone as Le Duc (the duke). He carried himself proudly and he and his wife sold from a big van parked in their regular place at the market. They were both well respected and liked by all the other dealers. They had always been very friendly to me and Helen. *Gitans* are often treated like outsiders and I believe that as we were foreigners, and immigrants, to boot, Le Duc was more helpful and sympathetic to us. If Brits living in France complain to me about 'immigrants', I enjoy pointing out that we ourselves are immigrants and that as such we should be more sympathetic.

I took a stroll up the road to buy a couple of croissants for breakfast and a *pain au céréal* for lunch. The bakery at Soumoulou opened early and sold an especially tasty *pain au céréal* which arrived hot in a small wooden box. Most of the French *boulangeries* bake their own loaves and patisseries on site in the shop. It was something you tended to take for granted. Once you've got your bread for the day in France, everything is all right with the world. Except I still couldn't stop worrying about where Serge was and if he was all right. It was always in the back of my mind.

I walked back to my pitch and began setting up my parasols and tables. It was getting lighter and a few traders were huddled in groups, chatting together. A young *gitan* I didn't recognise was making the early morning rounds, going from dealer to dealer, asking if they had any violins. As it happened I did have a pair of violins for sale. We had bought them in England on our last trip. They were fairly battered and we didn't think they were of any great value, unlike the Stradivarius that Serge had once bought at a sale in the Auvergne. We had paid very little for ours and without any knowledge of violins you tend to assume they are probably worthless. When he arrived at our stand I produced the pair of tatty black violin cases from the back of the van. He opened them, head down, looking at the violins closely, tightening the bows and checking the bodies of the instruments for cracks or any damage. He pointed out several deficiencies and seemed to be giving me the impression he didn't care much. I assumed he didn't want me to up the price. When he had finished his examination he asked how much. I made up a higher price than we wanted and he looked dubious. He pointed out that they would need some repair and offered a lower figure. I wasn't in the mood for haggling and agreed. It gave us a reasonable profit and that was good enough. He went off happy and I thought no more about it.

It was proving to be a good morning for customers. Chantal, the kindly woman who always stalled out next to me at Soumoulou, gave me the thumbs up. She had picked up this habit from me. I smiled and gave her the thumbs up back. I asked her to watch my stand for a minute and took a stroll over to where Serge used to stall out, just in case he was there. His place had been taken by Guy and Simone, an older French couple selling old copper and brassware. They hadn't been doing the markets long and the husband had told me he had purchased an industrial polishing machine which they'd set up in their garage at home. They enjoyed market life just as myself and Helen did. They bought all the old copper and brass they could lay their hands on, polished it up and presented it gleaming on their stand. It was like new lamps for old in the tale of Aladdin. They were doing well but we'd noticed that recently many of the long-standing regular *brocanteurs* had deregistered and stopped doing the professional antique markets. Instead they were selling at the *vide greniers* (car boot sales) alongside the *particulars* (private sellers) and amateur weekenders. This way they avoided the heavy monthly charges they were obliged to pay as registered professionals. Their places were being taken by retired couples with good pensions who had a taste for antiques and found working as *brocanteurs* enriched their lives – they were meeting people out in the fresh air and having fun. They were often successful as they were happy to sell things at cheaper prices and make less profit.

Guy and Simone had both worked as shop assistants in a department store in Bayonne all their lives. Guy had swept back grey hair, sported a pencil moustache and was always immaculately dressed. Simone had worked in women's fashion and was *très chic*. They were both charming and sold well to the public and other dealers, who would buy in bulk from them at a knock-down price and sell on their own stands for much more. Guy never complained about this. He once told me he liked polishing brass and copper in his garage. 'I look on it more as an enjoyable hobby,' he said. 'The more I sell, the happier I am... it's not difficult finding filthy brass and copper ornaments that need cleaning and polishing. People just throw them out. But if they saw the difference when they shine like gold after I've been at work, they wouldn't part with them so easily.' He was tickled pink with his new job. The various pots, pans and brass ornaments glittered seductively, positioned artfully on shelves in an impressive display.

Across the way I noticed Thibaut manhandling a huge provincial Louis XIV walnut armoire into position next to his stand. I went over to help him, although he didn't really need me. He was one of the few *brocanteurs* around strong enough to deal with these massive pieces of furniture on his own. This particular piece was magnificent. The wood gleamed with a beautiful honeyed glow. It was expertly crafted with pegged hand-cut solid planks of walnut. Pieces of furniture like this were much sought-after and he had no trouble selling them for a good price. I had heard his partner had just given birth to a baby girl and I offered him my congratulations. He was beaming, clearly delighted. 'She's beautiful,' he said.

'Have you decided on a name yet?' I asked.

'We both like the name Zoe.'

'I like that too,' I said.

'I think that's the one,' he said. He unlocked the door of the armoire and swung it open. It smelled sweet, of beeswax and polish. There were tiers of solid walnut shelving for stacking linen. Those old French craftsmen knew what they were doing when they made these armoires.

Visitors were beginning to arrive in droves in a pre-midday rush. I wished Thibaut *'merde'* (the French all say this instead of good luck, a bit like the theatrical 'break a leg') and crossed an adjacent aisle to head back to my stand. On the way I passed Reg stalled out in front of his caravan, which was pulled up alongside the exterior wall of the bullring. Bullrings are in most French towns and villages right across south-west France, and bullfighting is gaining in popularity, especially among the young. The Spanish in Catalonia have banned them but the French celebrate them. I personally think it is an unwelcome throwback to the arenas and blood sports of the Roman games. Helen and I both find the idea of making a spectacle of torturing and killing animals abhorrent. We are never able to forget, as many *brocantes* and fairs are situated in close proximity to the arenas. We've even been to some in the bullrings themselves, with bloodstains on the sand.

It certainly wasn't something that would have worried Reg, though. He came over and slapped me on the back. 'How's it going?'

'Not bad,' I said.

'I heard you did one of those *salons* up north. Any good, was it?' He rubbed his fingers together greedily.

'I don't think we'll be doing any more,' I said, wondering how he knew. 'It was OK.' I always try to avoid saying how well we did as it seems to make other dealers sick with jealousy.

'Whose big idea was it to do that then?'

I admitted Serge had suggested it. 'We shared a stand with him and Diddy,' I said.

'Well, that was your first big mistake then. I don't think Serge knows anything about that upmarket *salon* lark. He's a common-or-garden outdoor lad like the rest of us.'

'Actually, we're really worried about him,' I said. 'Something awful happened and we haven't seen or heard from him since.' I explained the whole story. How Anne-Marie had turned up and told Serge Diddy wasn't his real son and how devastated Serge had been.

Reg's attitude changed. 'Blimey! Poor bloke. He obviously loved that boy despite all his moaning about him. What a bummer.'

'He's disappeared,' I said. 'No one's seen hide nor hair of him. If you do see him, let me know, would you?'

'Course I will,' said Reg.

'We've been worried sick. He was in a terrible state... we thought he might have done something stupid.'

Rita emerged from the caravan with a fag in her mouth and a cup of tea in the other. She plonked the tea on the table in front of Reg. She smiled at me. 'Fancy a cuppa, John?'

'Thanks, but I better get back,' I said, looking around. There were more and more visitors arriving, parking in the square, thronging the market.

'You go,' said Reg. 'It's starting to liven up. I'll send Rita over with a cuppa for you later.'

He was right. The crowds were milling about. As I approached my stand I could see Chantal wrapping something and handing it to a customer. She pulled me to one side and counted out a wad of euros into my hand, delighted. 'I sold that set of tureens, full price,' she said. 'I refused to drop.'

'Marvellous!' I said. 'Thanks, Chantal, I owe you one.' She smiled and crossed back to her stand to deal with her own customers. This was one of the things I liked about working the French markets. Through touring around we had gradually got to know most of the dealers, and by and large they were a friendly bunch.

Algie strolled past my stand and, abnormally for him, spoke quite kindly. 'Reg told me about Serge. Poor bastard, so to speak!' He laughed out loud. 'But seriously, he's well out of that one if you ask me.' My stand was now thronged with customers. 'I'll leave you to it,' he said and wandered off.

I sold a nineteenth-century naval telescope to a collector and the English tea sets and cutlery were flying out. I barely had time to draw breath. Over the sea of heads I recognised an older couple who were regular customers of ours. They owned a hotel in Lourdes where Bernadette's grotto drew a huge number of visitors every year and this had made them very wealthy. The lady was a doll collector and she had come specifically to see if we had any that might interest her. I have never been that keen on dolls, but Helen had the knowledge and took the risk and we now had a bit of a name for them. I was surprised to discover that as we sold them for a profit I was beginning to change my attitude. Money makes things more appealing, I've found. I was learning about the different manufacturers and tried to admire the craftsmanship and the pretty blandness of their little faces. Some of them were quite sweet! I must be going soft in my old age.

The lady was excited as she examined an unusual antique French Limoges doll. Her husband stood by smiling – he clearly indulged her obsession. It didn't take her long to decide. She loved it and her husband handed the money over with a grin. I wrapped it carefully in bubble wrap to protect its fragile porcelain head and the pair of them went off happy.

As the morning went on I had four or five *gitans* come past and ask if I had any violins for sale. One of them even came through and started nosing around in the back of my van as if he didn't believe me before I persuaded him I had none. He wanted to know when I would be getting any more, and when I told him I didn't know he seemed quite disgruntled about it, like I might be lying.

The rush was beginning to ease up. Families were starting to stroll back to their cars. I was about to fetch my *pain au céréal* and some brie from the van to start my lunch when there was a shout and Le Duc came striding towards me. He looked annoyed and came between my tables and grabbed me by the arm.

'John, I thought you were my friend.' He was squeezing me and his voice was filled with emotion.

'I am,' I said. 'We are friends.'

'Well, you're supposed to do favours for your friends.'

'Of course,' I said hastily, hoping it wouldn't be some Herculean task.

'Next time you have any violins for sale, bring them to me first,' he said emphatically.

'OK, naturally I will,' I said, my heart sinking. 'I'll bring them to you first, I promise.'

'Right, don't ever forget.' He shook my hand firmly and walked off.

I sat down hard in the back of my van. It had dawned on me what this was all about. Le Duc was never insistent about anything. The violin I had sold to the young *gitan* earlier must have been worth much more than we realised. I imagined him going around bragging about how cheaply he had bought it from *l'idiot Anglais* and how much he was going to sell it for. That was the reason I had suddenly become of such interest to the *gitan* violin dealers. I felt sick. Because of our lack of knowledge I had made the most dreadful boo-boo. Ignorance in the antiques trade is never bliss. I was so depressed when the enormity of the mistake sunk in that I had to phone Helen and tell her about it.

'Oh well, never mind,' she said. 'These things happen.' I was often amazed at how philosophical she could be. 'But you sold the Limoges doll and made a profit and we've had a good morning,' she said. 'Try to look on the positive side.'

She was right. It was a sunny day, I had sold well and it was lunchtime. I sat looking at my beautiful *pain au céréal* in its lovely little wooden box and my hunk of brie cheese... but I had lost my appetite. That violin could have been worth a fortune. We'd seen them go for thousands at French auctions. I felt like a complete fool. And the young *gitan* would be going around feeling superior, crowing at my foolishness.

As I sat watching the crowds head off for *déjeuner* I was feeling miserable. How long had we been in this antiques lark? Surely I should have learnt to be more careful when selling an article with a potential high value. Priceless antiques still slipped through the hands of valuers everywhere, even in the auction houses. You couldn't always rely on them to spot the gems. That was one of the things that made this game exciting; the quest for that unexpected bargain among the general run-of-the-mill dross. No good, though, if you can't spot it. I ate my lunch listlessly and took a short siesta in the front of the van.

When I woke up there was a toddler standing across the way looking up at a teddy bear sitting on the end of my table. He was fascinated. I smiled as he held up one hand towards it. It wasn't a valuable one, not a Steiff or anything like that. I went and picked it up and bent down to show him. He was spellbound. I remembered the violin and shut my eyes, vowing never to be such an idiot again. The bear was a Chad Valley, made in England in the fifties. We got it in a lot with the doll I'd sold to the lady from Lourdes. If someone had given me a teddy when I was a kid, I would never have forgotten it. He could keep the bear. Why not? As soon as I'd made the decision and saw his pleasure my depression lifted. I felt good again.

Chantal called out, 'Bravo, John!'

I got down on my knees and played with him, wiggling the bear about, making it come to life, dancing it around from side to side like Sooty (my favourite... the original with Harry Corbett) and the little boy gasped with delight. I saw Chantal smiling and laughing next door. The boy held out his arms to me so sweetly, asking to hold the toy. I passed it to him and he clutched it, cuddling it up close to his chest. The look on his face was priceless... he really loved it. As I crouched down in the dirt a dog came up to the boy. It was a short-legged, rough-coated hunting dog with long floppy ears. The boy held the teddy out to show him and he nuzzled it. Something stirred in my memory. A bell rang. Where had I seen a dog like this before? It sauntered past the little boy, came straight up and looked at me with its soft brown eyes. I put my hand out and it licked me. Then it licked me again more enthusiastically and jumped up and pawed at me. Its tail was wagging like mad. I dropped down and rolled over and the dog jumped on me, licking my face and making me laugh. A small crowd had gathered and looked on, enjoying it as much as I was.

Then I recognised him. It was Robespierre – it had to be! But that was impossible. Robespierre was off somewhere on a yacht in the islands round Martinique with Angelique and Serge's real son, Adrien.

'He remembers you then?' I looked up from the ground and there was Serge standing outlined against the sun.

'Serge!' I was speechless.

'She came back, Johnny. It was Angelique I saw at the marina in Hendaye. She came back to France and brought my little Adrien and my darling Robespierre. This is Adrien.' He ruffled the boy's hair.

'But that's wonderful,' I said. I was on the edge of tears.

Robespierre licked my face as I got up.

'Adrien, *bonjour toi*!' He was cuddling his teddy.

'I've got Adrien for the weekend,' said Serge. 'Angelique's affair with her rich boyfriend fizzled out. He brought her back to France. She's given me back Robespierre and I can see Adrien whenever I like now.' His eyes were glistening.

'*Fantastique!*' I said. 'I can't wait to tell Helen... *C'est fantastique!*' And I meant it.

'Serge, I'm so pleased to see you.'

'And me you, Johnny... and me you.'

AND LIFE GOES ON...

I'm sitting outside our gingerbread house in the forest as I write this. It's quiet, just the soft sound of the wind through the pines. Helen puts out seed for the birds every day and the deer come and eat it secretly, soft shadows slipping through the trees. I hardly dare to breathe as I look out for them. I have to admit she was right about selling up and moving to the forest. It's absolutely wonderful here. The atmosphere is like nowhere else we've lived, though I don't believe anywhere could be so idyllic. There must be a catch somewhere.

We haven't sold our house yet and we've got a bridging loan hanging over our heads. We're crossing our fingers, hoping that someone won't mind a house next door to a *lotissement*. But I'm trying not to think about that now.

Helen and Angelique have renewed their friendship and Angelique's version of what happened in Martinique turns out to be completely different from Serge's. No surprise there then!

Serge is coming round to see us later. He's got his little Adrien for the weekend. He's a sweet little boy. It's nice to have Serge back and he's more like his old incorrigible self again. I have wondered what his cryptic comment about Bruno, *'pour lui la mayonnaise a tourné'*, meant. I've got a feeling I'm going to find out soon. But whatever happens I've promised Helen I'm going to stay out of trouble. When I tell her I won't get involved in whatever Serge suggests she smiles and says, 'Mmmm, yes dear...'

John Dummer

SERGE BASTARDE
ate my
BAGUETTE

ON the ROAD
in the
REAL RURAL
FRANCE

SERGE BASTARDE
BROCANTEUR

SERGE BASTARDE ATE MY BAGUETTE
On the Road in the Real Rural France

John Dummer

ISBN: 978 1 84024 770 1   Paperback   £8.99

It would have been churlish to have refused his invitation to accompany him on a trip out in the country to 'forage for hidden treasures'. If the truth be known, I secretly couldn't resist the novelty of passing time with a bloke called Serge Bastarde.

When John decamps to France to start up as an antiques dealer, he doesn't count on meeting Serge Bastarde. The lovable rogue and *brocanteur* offers to teach John the tricks of the trade in return for help in a series of breathtakingly unscrupulous schemes.

As the pair trawl through markets and farmhouses, they get into more than their fair share of scrapes: whether they're conning hearty lunches from unsuspecting old peasants, manufacturing fake collectibles or losing a Stradivarius to gypsies.

Filled with eccentric characters, high jinks and unlikely adventures, this is a hilarious romp through the real rural France.

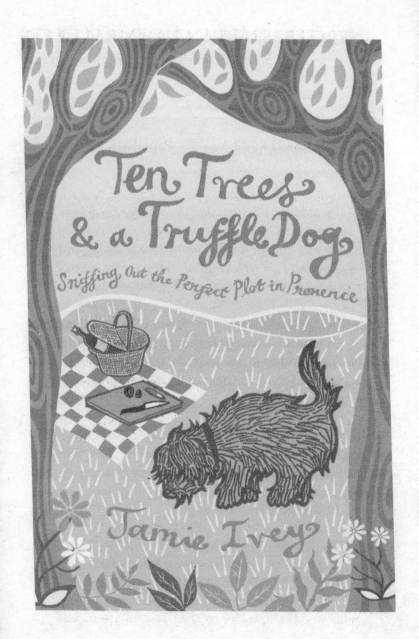

Ten Trees & a Truffle Dog

Sniffing Out the Perfect Plot in Provence

Jamie Ivey

TEN TREES AND A TRUFFLE DOG
Sniffing Out the Perfect Plot in Provence

Jamie Ivey

ISBN: 978 1 84953 238 9   Paperback   £8.99

Snuffle sniffed the bowl, looked plaintively up at me, and then began to whine. Why had I wrecked a perfectly good meal, a meal he'd been waiting for all day, by shaving truffle all over it? I looked disdainfully back at him – of all the dogs in the world why did I have to get lumbered with one stubborn enough to resist the supposedly irresistible scent of truffles?

The plot of land was perfect, affordable and came with a plantation of truffle oaks. Having exchanged London life for Provence, started a wine business and a family, here was a chance for Jamie and his wife to realise the final part of their dream. All they needed now was to build a house – and train a dog. But would they survive the secretive world of truffle hunters?

'The best relocation book I have read and a smashing book by any standards… It kept me up half the night.'
Terry Darlington, author of *Narrow Dog to Carcasonne*

'The scents and flavours of Provence waft and spill from every delicious page. Read it and salivate.'
Antony Woodward, author of *The Garden in the Clouds*

Tout Sweet

Hanging up my High Heels for a New Life in France

KAREN WHEELER

NEW LIFE

LOVE?

TOUT SWEET
Hanging Up My High Heels for a New Life in France

Karen Wheeler

ISBN: 978 1 84024 761 9   Paperback   £8.99

In her mid-thirties, fashion editor Karen has it all: a handsome boyfriend, a fab flat in west London and an array of gorgeous shoes. But when Eric leaves, she hangs up her Manolos and waves goodbye to her glamorous city lifestyle to go it alone in a run-down house in rural Poitou-Charentes, central western France.

Acquiring a host of new friends and unsuitable suitors, she learns that true happiness can be found in the simplest of things – a bike ride through the countryside on a summer evening, or a kir or three in a neighbour's courtyard.

Perfect summer reading for anyone who dreams of chucking away their BlackBerry in favour of real blackberrying and downshifting to France.

'an hilarious account of a fashion guru who swaps
Prada for paintbrushes and Pineau in rural France'
MAIL ON SUNDAY Travel

Have you enjoyed this book?
If so, why not write a review on your favourite website?

If you're interested in finding out more about our travel books
friend us on Facebook at **Summersdale Traveleditor**
and follow us on Twitter: @SummersdaleGO

Thanks very much for buying this Summersdale book.

www.summersdale.com